APPLE GROWING

M.C. BURRITT

Contents

PREFACE 7
CHAPTER I THE OUTLOOK FOR THE GROWING OF APPLES 8
CHAPTER II PLANNING FOR THE ORCHARD.....................................13
CHAPTER III PLANTING AND GROWING THE ORCHARD 23
CHAPTER IV PRUNING THE TREES...35
CHAPTER V CULTIVATION AND COVER CROPPING 44
CHAPTER VI MANURING AND FERTILIZING 54
CHAPTER VII INSECTS AND DISEASES AFFECTING THE APPLE 63
CHAPTER VIII THE PRINCIPLES AND PRACTICE OF SPRAYING....73
CHAPTER IX HARVESTING AND STORING 86
CHAPTER X MARKETS AND MARKETING 96
CHAPTER XI SOME HINTS ON RENOVATING OLD ORCHARDS ...103
CHAPTER XII THE COST OF GROWING APPLES 110

APPLE GROWING

BY

M.C. BURRITT

PREFACE

In the preparation of this book I have tried to keep constantly before me the conditions of the average farm in the Northeastern States with its small apple orchard. It has been my aim to set down only such facts as would be of practical value to an owner of such a farm and to state these facts in the plain language of experience. This book is in no sense intended as a final scientific treatment of the subject, and if it is of any value in helping to make the fruit department of the general farm more profitable the author will be entirely satisfied.
The facts herein set down were first learned in the school of practical experience on the writer's own farm in Western New York. They were afterwards supplemented by some theoretical training and by a rather wide observation of farm orchard conditions and methods in New York, Pennsylvania, the New England States and other contiguous territory. These facts were first put together in something like their present form in the winter of 1909-10, when the writer gave a series of lectures on Commercial Fruit Growing to the Short Courses in Horticulture at Cornell University. These lectures were revised and repeated in 1910-11 and are now put in their present form.
The author's sincere thanks are due to Professor C.S. Wilson, of the Department of Pomology at Cornell University, for many valuable facts and suggestions used in this book, and for a careful reading of the manuscript. He is also under obligations to Mr. Roy D. Anthony of the same Department for corrections and suggestions on the chapters on Insects and Diseases and on Spraying.

M.C. BURRITT.
Hilton, N.Y.February, 1912.

CHAPTER I
THE OUTLOOK FOR THE GROWING OF APPLES

The apple has long been the most popular of our tree fruits, but the last few years have seen a steady growth in its appreciation and use. This is probably due in a large measure to a better knowledge of its value and to the development of new methods of preparation for consumption. Few fruits can be utilized in as many ways as can the apple. In addition to the common use of the fresh fruit out of hand and of the fresh, sweet juice as cider, this "King of Fruits" can be cooked, baked, dried, canned, and made into jellies and other appetizing dishes, to enumerate all of which would be to prepare a list pages long. Few who have tasted once want to be without their apple sauce and apple pies in season, not to mention the crisp, juicy specimens to eat out of hand by the open fireplace in the long winter evenings. Apples thus served call up pleasant memories to most of us, but only recently have the culinary possibilities of the apple, especially as a dessert fruit, been fully realized.

It is doubtless this realization of its great adaptability, together with its long season, which have brought the apple into so great demand of late. It is possible to have apples on the table in some form the year round. The first summer apples are almost always with us before the bottom of the Russet barrel is reached. Or, should the fresh fruit be too expensive or for some reason fail altogether, the housewife can fall back on the canned and dried fruit which are almost as good.

The tendency in the price of this staple fruit has been constantly upward during the last decade. Many people are greatly surprised when the fact that apples cost more than oranges is called to their attention. The increase in consumption, due to the greater variety of ways of preparing the apple for use, has undoubtedly been an important factor in this higher price. But at least an equally important factor is the marked decrease in the supply of this fruit. To those who are not familiar with the facts, the great falling off in production which the figures show will be no less than startling.

PRODUCTION OF APPLES IN BARRELS IN THE UNITED STATES FROM 1896 TO 1910

1896	69,070,000
1897	41,530,000
1898	28,570,000
1899	37,460,000
1900	56,820,000

Total crop for five years	233,450,000
Average crop for five years	46,690,000
1901	26,970,000
1902	46,625,000
1903	42,626,000
1904	45,360,000
1905	24,310,000

Total crop for five years	185,891,000

Average crop for five years	37,178,200
1906	38,280,000
1907	29,540,000
1908	25,850,000
1909	25,415,000
1910	23,825,000
Total crop for five years	142,910,000

Average crop for five years	28,582,000

Estimates of 1896, 1897, and 1898 from "Better Fruit," Vol. 5, No. 5. All other years from the estimates of the "American Agriculturist."

It will thus be seen that the apple crop of 1910 was 45,245,000 barrels less than that of 1896, and that during the whole period of fifteen years the decline has been regular. The average annual crop of the five year period ending with 1905 was 9,511,800 barrels less than the average annual crop of the preceding five years ending with 1900, and correspondingly the annual average crop of the last five years, ending with 1910, was 8,596,200 barrels less than that of the second five year period. Comparing the first and the last five year periods, we find that the crop of the last was 18,108,000 barrels less than that of the first. These facts alone are enough to explain the higher price of this fruit during the last ten years.

HEAVY PLANTINGS.--Moreover, it should be further noted that this falling off in the apple crop has been in the face of the heaviest plantings ever known in this country. During the last ten years old fruit growing regions like western New York have practically doubled their orchard plantings. Careful figures gathered by the New York State Agricultural College in an orchard survey of Monroe County show that 4,972 more trees (21,289 in all) were planted in one representative township during the five year period from 1904 to 1908 inclusive than were ever planted in any other equal period in its history. New fruit regions like the Northwestern States and a large part of the Shenandoah valley of Virginia have been developed by heavy plantings. These three are all great commercial sections. To them we might add thousands of orchards which are scattered all over the Northern and Eastern States, from Michigan to Maine and from Maine to north Georgia.

It is doubtful, however, if these scattered plantings have made good the older trees which have died out. Scarcely a season passes that hundreds of these old veteran trees are not blown down or badly broken. Every wind takes its toll. After one of these windstorms in Southern New York the writer estimated that at least twenty per cent of all the standing old apple trees had been destroyed or badly broken. In the commercial regions only a small part of the new plantings have yet come to bearing and even here these probably do not much more than make good the losses of old trees. So that on the whole, heavy as our plantings have been, it is extremely doubtful if they have very much more than made good the losses of the older trees throughout the country. It is a fact worthy of note that this talk of over-planting the apple has been going on for over thirty years, and while the timid ones talked those who had faith in the business and the courage of their convictions planted apples and reaped golden harvests while their neighbors still talked of over-planting.

Whether or not it is true that we have over-planted the apple, it must be admitted that at the present time the demand is so much greater than the supply that the poorer of our people cannot afford to use apples commonly, and that no class of farmer in the Northeastern

States is more prosperous than the fruit growers. The new plantings must of necessity begin to bear and become factors in the market very slowly. Meanwhile the great opportunity of the present lies in making the most possible out of the older orchards which are already in bearing. Practically all of these old farm orchards which can present a fairly clean bill of health, and in which the varieties are desirable, can with a small amount of well directed effort be put to work at once and during the next ten years or more of their life time, they may be made to add a substantial income to that of the general farm. Now is a time of opportunity for the owner of the small farm apple orchard.

FUTURE OF APPLE GROWING.--In the writer's opinion the future of apple growing in the United States is likely to shape itself largely in the great commercial regions. As these become more and more developed and as the industry becomes more specialized the farmer who is merely growing apples as a side line, except where he is delivering directly to a special or a local market, will be crowded out. Here as elsewhere it will be a case of the survival of the fittest. In the production of apples commercially those growers who can produce the best article the most cheaply are bound to win out in the end.

It would, therefore, seem to be advisable for the general farmer to plant apples only under two conditions; first, when he has a very favorable location and site and plants heavily enough to make it worth while to have the equipment and skilled labor necessary to make the enterprise a success, and second, when he can market his fruit directly in a local market. It would appear that the immediate future of apple growing in the United States lies in the small farm orchard as well as in the commercial orchards, but that the more distant future lies in the commercial orchard except where special conditions surround the farm.

CHAPTER II
PLANNING FOR THE ORCHARD

LOCATION.--Having decided that under certain conditions the planting of an apple orchard will prove a profitable venture, and having ascertained that those conditions prevail on your farm, the next step will be to determine the best location on the farm for the orchard. In choosing this location it will be well to keep in mind the relative importance of the orchard in the scheme of farm management. If the orchard is merely a source of home supply, naturally it will not require as important a position on the farm as will be the case if it is expected to yield a larger share of the farm income. If the relatively large net income per acre which it is possible to obtain from an apple orchard is to be secured, the best possible location is demanded.

Contrary to the common ideas and practice of the past, the orchard should not be put upon the poorest soil on the farm. The best orchards occupy the best soils, although fairly good results are often obtained on poor or medium soils. The relative importance which is attached to the orchard enterprise must also govern the choice of soil. If apples are to be a prominent crop they should be given the preference as to soil; if not, they may be given a place in accordance with what is expected of them.

SOILS.--In general, the apple prefers a rather strong soil, neither very heavy nor very light. Subsoil is rather more important than surface soil, although the latter should be friable and easily worked. The apple follows good timber successfully. Heavy clay soils are apt to be too cold, compact, and wet; light sandy soils too loose and dry. A medium clay loam or a gravelly clay loam, underlaid by a somewhat heavier but fairly open clay subsoil is thought to be the best soil for apples. Broadly considered, medium loams are best. The lighter the soil the better will be the color of the fruit as a rule, and so, also, the heavier the soil and the more nitrogen and moisture it holds the greater the tendency to poorly colored fruit. In the same way light soils give poorer wood and foliage growth as compared with the large rank leaves and wood of trees on heavy, rich soils.

VARIETAL SOIL PREFERENCES are beginning to be recognized. We cannot go into these in detail in this brief discussion. A few suggestions regarding standard varieties must suffice. Medium to light loams or heavy sandy loams, underlaid by slightly heavier loams or clay loams, are preferred by the Baldwin, which has a wider soil adaptation than practically any other variety. Baldwin soils should dry quickly after a rain. Rhode Island Greening requires a rather rich, moist, but well drained soil, containing an abundance of organic matter. A light to heavy silty loam, underlaid by a silty clay loam, is considered best.

Northern Spy is very exacting in its soil requirements. A medium loam, underlaid by a heavy loam or a light clay loam, is excellent. Heavy soils give the Spy a greasy skin. Light soils cause the tree to grow upright and to bear fruit of poor flavor. The King likes a soil slightly lighter than the best Greening soils, but retentive of moisture. Hubbardson will utilize the sandiest soil of any northern variety, preferring rich, fine, sandy loams.

The particular location of the apple orchard is largely a matter of convenience. It should be remembered, however, that the apple requires much and constant attention, therefore the orchard should be convenient of access. The product is rather bulky, so that the haul to the highway should be as short as possible. Other conditions being equally good there, the common location near the buildings and highway is best.

THE SITE OF THE ORCHARD is a more important matter. Two essentials should be kept in mind, good air drainage and a considerable elevation. Although it is not so apparent and therefore less thought about, cold air runs down hill the same as water. Being heavier, it falls to the surface of the land, flowing out through the water channels and settling in pockets and depressions. Warm air, being lighter, rises. It is desirable to avoid conditions of stagnant air or cold air pockets where frost and fogs are liable to occur. A free movement of air, especially a draining away of cold air, is best secured by an elevation. Fifty to one hundred feet, or sometimes less, is usually sufficient, especially where there is good outlet below. Frosts occur in still, clear air and these conditions occur most frequently in the lower areas.

Aspect or slope requires less attention. Southern exposures are warm and hasten bud development and opening in spring. Northern exposures are cold and retard the blossoming period. It is usually advisable to plant the apple on the colder slopes which hold it back in spring until all danger of late frosts is past. Northeast exposures are best as a general rule. Choose a slope away from the prevailing wind if possible. If this is impracticable it is often advisable to plant a wind break of pine, spruce, or a quick, thick growing native tree to protect the orchard from heavy winds.

A large body of water is an important modifier of climate. Warming up more slowly in the spring, it retards vegetation by slowly giving up its cold. Vice versa, cooling more slowly in the fall giving up its heat wards off the early frosts. It is therefore desirable to locate near such bodies of water if possible. Their influence varies according to their size and depth, and the distance of the orchard from them. Good examples of this influence are the Chautauqua Grape Belt on the eastern shore of Lake Erie and the Western New York Apple Belt on the south shore of Lake Ontario.

Professor Brackett has well summed up the whole question: "The selection of the soil and site for the apple orchard is not governed by any arbitrary rule," he says. "All farms do not afford the best soils or exposures for orchards. The owners of such as do not are unfortunate, yet they should not feel discouraged to the extent of not planting trees and caring for them afterward." There are a number of factors which influence not only a person who wishes to locate, but one already located, either favorably or unfavorably. About these even the most intelligent orchardists often differ. We have only laid down general principles and given opinions. Here as elsewhere application is a matter of judgment.

VARIETIES.--A proper soil and a good location and site having been selected, the next important question to be decided is the varieties to be planted. So much and so variable advice is given on this question that many persons are at a loss as to what to plant and too often decide the matter by planting the wrong varieties. Rightly viewed, the question of varieties is a comparatively simple one. Personal preference, tempered by careful study of certain factors and good judgment, are all that are required. Beginners, especially, are too apt to rely entirely on another's opinion. The only safe way is to learn the facts and then decide for yourself.

We have already indicated that soil is a determinant in the choice of varieties. This should be absolute. It is very unwise to try to grow any variety on a soil where experience has shown that it does not do well. The experience of your neighbors is the best guide in this respect.

The limitations of climate should also be carefully heeded. An apple may be at its best in one latitude or one situation and at its worst in another. Find out from experienced growers in your region, or from your State Experiment Station what varieties are best adapted climatically to the place where you live. It is an excellent rule never to plant a variety that you cannot grow at least as well as any one else, or still better, to plant a variety that you can grow better than anyone else. Grow something that not everyone can grow. Do not try to produce more of a variety of which there is already an over supply.

A few examples may make this more clear. Western New York is the home of the Baldwin, the Twenty Ounce and the King. Albemarle Pippins grown on the eastern slope of the Blue Ridge are famous. The Spitzenburg appears at its best in the Northwest. The Northern Spy, the McIntosh, and the Fameuse are not to be excelled as they are grown in the Champlain Valley, in Vermont, or in Maine. To attempt to compete with these sections in the growing of these varieties, except under equally favorable conditions, would be foolish. Your section probably grows some varieties to perfection. Find out what these varieties are and plant them.

All these are general factors to be observed which cannot be specifically settled without knowing the soil and particular locality. Certain other factors governing the choice of varieties can be more definitely outlined. If the prospective orchardist will get these factors thoroughly in mind and apply them with judgment mistakes in planting should be much more rare. The more important ones are: The purpose for which the fruit is intended to be used, whether for the general market, a dessert or fancy trade, or for culinary and general table use; whether the trees are to be permanent and long lived, or temporary and used as fillers; whether the earliest possible income is desired or whether this is to be secondary to the future development of the orchard; whether the stock of the particular variety is strong or weak growing; whether the variety is high, medium, or low as to quality; and whether the market is to be local, distant, or export.

The following tables were originally compiled by Professor C.S. Wilson of Cornell University. They have been slightly revised and modified for our purpose. We believe that they are essentially correct and that they will be a safe guide for the reader to follow in his selection of varieties:

GENERAL MARKET APPLES
COMMERCIAL

Baldwin
Ben Davis
Hubbardson
Northern Spy
King
Rome Beauty
Oldenburg
Alexander
Twenty Ounce
Winesap
York Imperial

DESSERT OR FANCY TRADE
BOX WELL

McIntosh
Northern Spy
Fameuse
Wagener
Grimes Golden
Yellow Newton
Red Canada
King
Sutton
Hubbardson
Esopus Spitzenburg

CULINARY AND GENERAL TABLE USE

Rhode Island Greening   Grimes Golden
Gravenstein   Twenty Ounce
Newtown   Yellow Bellflower
Alexander   Oldenburg
Tolman Sweet   Sweet Winesap

GOOD PERMANENT   GOOD TEMPORARY
TREES   TREES--FILLERS

Baldwin   McIntosh
Rhode Island Greening   Wealthy
Northern Spy   Wagener
McIntosh   Rome Beauty
*King   Oldenburg
*Twenty Ounce   Jonathan
*Hubbardson   Alexander
Alexander   Twenty Ounce
Rome Beauty   Hubbardson

  * When this variety is set as a permanent tree it should be top
    worked on a hardier stock, such as Northern Spy.

Age at which variety may be expected to begin to fruit. (Add two years
for a paying crop).

FIVE YEARS OR UNDER

Rome Beauty
Oldenburg
Maiden Blush
Wagener
Yellow Newton
McIntosh
Fameuse
King
Rhode Island Gr.
Twenty Ounce
Winesap

EIGHT YEARS AND UP

Esopus Spitzenburg
Fall Pippin
Golden Russet
Northern Spy
Baldwin
Gravenstein
Tolman Sweet

ESPECIALLY HARDY STOCKS

Northern Spy
Tolman Sweet
Ben Davis
Baldwin
Fameuse
Winter Banana

POOR RATHER WEAK GROWERS*

King
Twenty Ounce
Esopus Spitzenburg
Hubbardson
Grimes Golden
Sutton
Canada Red

* Other varieties are medium.

HIGH IN QUALITY

McIntosh
Esopus Spitzenburg
Northern Spy
Newtown
Gravenstein

LOCAL OR PEDDLER'S VARIETIES

Rhode Island Greening
Wealthy
McIntosh
Fameuse
Tolman Sweet

Red Canada
Fameuse
Grimes Golden
Hubbardson
Rhode Island Greening

Grimes Golden
Jonathan

GOOD GENERAL MARKET VARIETIES

Baldwin
Rhode Island
King
Twenty Ounce
McIntosh
Hubbardson
Northern Spy

MEDIUM TO POOR QUALITY

Ben Davis
Oldenburg
Rome Beauty
Roxbury Russet

GOOD EXPORT VARIETIES

Baldwin
Ben Davis
Northern Spy

Newtown
Esopus Spitzenburg
Jonathan

Only the best and most common varieties for the more northern latitudes have been included in this list as it would make it too cumbersome to classify all our known varieties. It must be remembered that this is not an arbitrary classification and that it is made as a guide to indicate to the reader the general characteristics of the variety. It should be used as such and not taken literally. The characters of the different varieties grade into each other. For example, the McIntosh is very high and the Ben Davis is very low in quality but the King and the Twenty Ounce are neither very good nor very poor, but midway between.

We must again remind the reader that the choice of varieties is a matter of judgment, tempered by the facts regarding them. One who is not capable of rendering such judgment after studying his conditions and the characteristics and requirements of leading varieties had better stay out of the apple business entirely, as he will often be called on for the exercise of good judgment in caring for the orchard. The facts here given are intended as suggestive. The reader who desires to know more of a particular variety will do well to consult Beach's "Apples of New York," published by the Geneva Experiment Station.

CHAPTER III
PLANTING AND GROWING THE ORCHARD

The proper soil, site, and location having been selected, the solution of the problems of orchard management is only just begun, although a good start has certainly been made. Farm management brings constantly to one's attention new problems and new phases of old problems, whatever the type of farming. The skill with which these problems are met and a solution found for them determines the success or failure of the farm manager. To some men the details of the orchard business offer the greatest obstacles, while to others it is the general relationship of one detail to another which is difficult. Both are essentials of good management. If we are able in this chapter to remove some of these minor difficulties and at the same time indicate the correct relationships we will have accomplished our purpose.

As we come now to the actual plans for planting our orchard many questions come up for answer. When shall I plant? Where and of whom shall I purchase my trees? How old should they be? Is it wise to use fillers or temporary trees, and if so, what kind? How far apart should the trees be planted and how many are required for an acre? What arrangement of the trees is most advisable? How should the ground be prepared? What is the best method of setting? When the trees are planted should they be inter-cropped, and if so, with what? How should the young trees be handled and cared for? He who would be a successful orchardist must endeavor to answer these questions.

WHEN TO PLANT.--The question of fall or spring planting is a less important one with a comparatively hardy fruit like the apple than it is with a more tender fruit like the peach. Apples may safely be planted in the fall when soils are well drained and when the young trees are well matured, both of which are very important if winter injury is to be avoided. Fall planting has several distinct advantages. During the winter fall planted trees become well established in the soil which enables them to start root growth earlier in the spring. Consequently the young trees are better able to endure droughts. In the fall the weather is usually more settled and there is better opportunity to plant under favorable conditions than in the unsettled weather of spring. It is usually possible, too, to get a better selection of trees at the nursery in the fall because most of the trees are not sold until midwinter.

Still the fact remains that the common practice of spring planting is the more conservative course. There is always danger of getting immature trees in the fall, and of winter injury to fall planted trees. Trees may be set in the fall any time after the buds are mature which is usually after October 1st to 18th in the latitude of New York. They should not be pruned back in the fall, as this invites winter killing of the uppermost buds. The question of available time must also be considered. On some farms fall offers more time; on others, spring. To sum up the matter, plant at the most convenient time, providing the conditions are favorable.

WHERE TO BUY.--But one rule as to where to buy trees can be laid down. Buy where you can secure the best trees and where you can be sure of the most reliable and honest dealers. Beware of the tree agent, who has been guilty of more dishonesty and misrepresentation than almost any other traveling agent. Buy of a salesman under one condition only, that he prove to you that he is the bona fide representative of a

well-known and reputable nursery firm, and then make your order
subject to investigation of the firm's standing and finding it as
represented.

The safest course is usually to purchase of your home nurseryman with
whose standing and honesty you are familiar, and whose trees you can
personally inspect. Such a man has a reputation at stake and will have
an object in keeping your trade. Moreover, you will save freight,
secure fresher stock with less liability of injury in handling, and
get trees grown under your own conditions. If stock is purchased away
from home it is better to get it at a nursery in a more southern
latitude in order to secure trees of better growth.

All trees should be purchased in the late summer or early fall when
the nurseryman has a full list of varieties and you can get the pick
of his stock. Select a well grown mature tree two years old from the
bud. One year old trees are preferred by many and if well grown and at
least five feet high they are probably best. But a one year old tree
is rather more delicate, requiring careful handling and intelligent
training. Unless a person buys from a southern nursery and is an
expert in handling trees, the two year old tree is to be preferred,
but a skilful grower can make a more satisfactory tree from a one year
old seedling.

The average buyer must depend largely on his nurseryman for getting
trees true to name, which is the reason for laying so much emphasis on
purchasing from an honest dealer. Some nurserymen guarantee their
varieties to be true to name, and all ought to do so. Buyers should
demand it. The seeds of the apple rarely come true to the variety
planted. They are therefore usually budded on one year old seedlings
imported from France. Sometimes they are whole or piece root grafted
which is equally as good a method of propagation.

It is possible for a man to grow and bud or graft his own seedlings, but hardly advisable for the average small grower or general farmer, as it is usually expensive when done on a small scale and requires considerable skill. Always buy a high grade tree. Seconds are often equally as good as firsts when they are simply smaller as a result of crowding in the nursery row. A tree which is second grade because of being stunted, crooked, or poorly grown should never be set. Thirds are seldom worth considering at any price.

FILLERS.--Whether or not the planter of an apple orchard should use fillers is a question which he alone must decide. In the writer's opinion there are more advantages than disadvantages in so doing, but we must state both sides of the question and let the reader judge for himself. The term "filler" is one used to designate a tree planted in the orchard for the temporary purpose of profitably occupying the space between the permanent trees while these are growing and not yet in bearing. Fillers make a more complete use of the land, bringing in larger as well as quicker returns from it, three distinct advantages. (See Chapter XII, The Cost of Growing Apples.) On the other hand, objections to their use are that they are often left in so long that they crowd and seriously injure the permanent trees, and that their care often requires different operations and at different times from the other trees, such as spraying, which may result in injury to the permanent trees in the orchard.

Trees used as fillers for apples should have two important characteristics; they should be rapid, vigorous growers and should come into bearing at a very early age. Two kinds of fillers are available, those of the same species, which may be either dwarf or standard trees, and those of a different species, of which peaches and plums, and possibly pears, are the best adapted. Dwarf trees may be dismissed from our plans with the statement that they have rarely proved profitable under ordinary conditions, as they are much more difficult to grow than standards and when grown they have but few advantages over them. The varieties of standard apples which are advisable as fillers have been indicated in Chapter II.

The use of peaches and the Japanese plums, both of which make excellent fillers because they grow rapidly and come to heavy bearing quickly, is limited to their soil and climatic adaptation. They are adapted to the lighter phases of soil and the more moderate climates and under other conditions are impracticable. On heavier soils and in more rigorous climates the European plums and the more rapid and early bearing pears, such as the Keiffer, make fairly good fillers.

On the whole, the writer is inclined to advise the use of fillers in the general farm orchard. Quicker returns from an investment of this nature, which is usually heavy and which at best must be put off several years, are very important. Under careful and intelligent management the objections to their use are easily overcome.

SPACING AND ARRANGEMENT OF TREES.--The distance apart of planting depends on the variety planted. Close headed, upright growing trees may be planted closer together than spreading varieties. Some varieties grow larger than others, and the same variety may vary in size on different soils. It is seldom advisable to plant standard apple trees in the latitude of New York closer than thirty feet, or farther apart than fifty feet. Trees of the nature of Twenty Ounce and Oldenburg (Dutchess) should be planted from thirty-two to thirty-six feet apart, while Baldwins, Rhode Island Greenings, and Northern Spies represent the other extreme and will require forty, and sometimes fifty feet of space. The method and thoroughness of pruning influences the size of trees greatly, and hence the distance at which It is necessary to set them.

Varieties top worked on other stocks have a tendency to grow more upright and may be set closer together. It should be remembered in this connection that the roots of a tree extend considerably beyond the spread of the branches. From thirty-five to forty feet is a good average distance and trees should be trained so as to occupy this space and no more. Where fillers are used the latter distance is best, as the twenty feet apart at which the trees will then stand is close enough for any standard variety.

RECTANGULAR.--The method of setting or the arrangement of the trees will greatly influence the number of trees which may be put upon an acre and the distance apart of the trees in the row. The most common method in the past has been the regular square or rectangular method, e.g., trees forty by forty feet, or forty by fifty feet, and rows at right angles, and this is still preferred by many. It is easy to lay out an orchard on this plan and there is less liability of making mistakes. It is best adapted to regular fields with right angle corners, especially where the orchard is to be cropped with a regular rotation. All tillage operations are most easily performed in orchards set on this plan.

A slight modification of this arrangement which is often advisable, especially where fillers are used, is to set a tree in the center of the square. The trees then stand like the five spots of a domino, and the shortest distance between trees will be about twenty-seven feet when the trees in the regular rows are forty by forty feet apart. This plan practically doubles the number of trees which can be set on an acre.

HEXAGONAL OR TRIANGULAR.--Another method of arrangement of the trees
which is becoming more and more popular is the hexagonal or triangular system. More trees can be planted on an acre by this plan than by any

other, it being very economical of space. It makes all adjacent trees equally distant from each other and is really a system of equilateral triangles. This plan is better adapted to small areas and especially to irregular ones, and should be employed where land is expensive and culture very intensive. It is more difficult to set an orchard after this method without error, and it is open to the objection of inconvenience in cultural operations. Most people forget that while the rows running cornerwise in a rectangular or square field set after this plan may be a standard distance apart, yet the right angle rows (not trees) in which it may be more convenient to work are actually much closer together.

The best plan to follow to get the rows of trees straight on a level field is what is known as the outside stake method. This plan requires the placing of a row of stakes on each of the four sides of the field where the trees are to be set and usually about two rows each way through the middle. For this purpose ordinary building laths are best, about one hundred and fifty laths, or three bundles, being required for five acres, which is as large a unit as can be set at once by this plan.

First, determine the distance from the road or fence to the first tree row, which would be at least eighteen feet to allow for turning the teams, and establish base lines on each side of the field at right angles to each other.

Second, beginning at the given distance from the side of the field, set up a row of stakes along these base lines at the exact distance apart at which the trees are to be set and about half way between the fence and the first right angle row. Do the same on all sides of the field.

Third, by sighting across the field from one end stake to the other the cross rows of stakes can be set through the middle of the field. These should be about six or eight rods apart, and care should be used to avoid setting them where they will interfere with the sighting of the right angle rows. This plan has the great merit of enabling the entire orchard to be set without moving a stake, as no stake stands where a tree is to be set. If the trees are set exactly where the sight lines cross at right angles and if all rows are an equal distance apart, the rows will be perfectly straight.

On rough or rolling land this plan does not work well. Here more simple methods, though requiring more time, must be used. Lines drawn with a cord or marked across the field with a corn planter answer well for small areas. Poles of the right length are often used to good advantage. In setting trees after the hexagonal plan an equilateral triangle made of light poles or wire is probably best, especially on small rough areas, as it is very accurate, simple, and quite rapid. Some men prefer to make measurements and set a stake at every point where a tree is to be placed. In these cases a simple device locates the original stakes after the hole has been dug. A light board about six feet long with a notch in the center and holes with pegs in them at each end is placed with the notch at the stake. One end is then swung round and the hole dug. When the end is replaced on its peg the tree set in the hole should rest in the notch where the original stake did.

The following table shows the number of trees required per acre at different distances for the square or rectangular method and for the hexagonal method.

	Sq.	Hex.		Sq.	Hex.
12 x 12	302	344	24 x 24	75	80
12 x 15	242	...	24 x 30	60	..
15 x 15	193	224	30 x 30	48	56
15 x 18	161	...	30 x 36	40	..
15 x 20	145	...	33 x 33	40	46
15 x 30	96	...	30 x 48	30	..
18 x 18	134	156	30 x 60	24	..
18 x 20	121	...	36 x 36	33	39
20 x 20	108	124	40 x 40	27	31
20 x 30	72	...	40 x 50	21	..

It will be noted that the hexagonal plan allows the setting of from four to forty trees more per acre than the square plan, even when the trees are set the same distance apart. This is the great advantage of this plan over the square. Filling an orchard one way, i.e., between the permanent row, in one direction only, practically doubles the trees which can be set on an acre; filling both ways quadruples the number.

PREPARATION OF SOIL.--The previous condition and treatment of a soil for an orchard are important. If the soil has been in a good rotation of field crops, including some cultivated crops, it should be in prime condition for the trees. Old pastures and meadows should be plowed up, cropped, and cultivated for a year or two before setting to obtain the best and quickest results. If one is in a hurry, however, this may be done after setting the trees. Good results are sometimes obtained by setting trees right among the stumps on recently cleared timberland. Where no stiff sod has formed the trees start quickly in the rich soil.

The best immediate treatment of land preparatory to setting the trees should be such as to place the soil in good tilth. Deep plowing, thorough cultivation, and the application of liberal amounts of manure--twelve to fifteen loads per acre--are the most effective means of doing this. The best crop immediately to precede trees is clover. Sometimes an application of one thousand five hundred to two thousand pounds of lime will help to insure a stand of clover and at the same time improve the physical condition of the soil. Fall plowing is a good practice on the medium loams and more open soils, but on the heavy clays spring plowing is to be preferred, as when plowed in the fall these soils puddle and become hard to handle. Care should always be taken to keep the orchard well furrowed out as standing water is decidedly inimical to satisfactory tree-growth. Tile draining is frequently advisable.

INTERCROPPING.--The question of intercropping a young orchard is one to be carefully considered. As it is often practiced it is very injurious to the orchard, but it is possible to manage crops so as to be of very little harm to the trees. While the practice may be inadvisable in many commercial orchards, yet on a general farm we should by all means think that it was the right thing to do. Certain facts must be remembered, however, which have a bearing on the subject.

Trees are a crop, as much as corn or grass. If we grow a crop between the tree rows we must remember that we are double cropping the land and that it must be fed and cared for accordingly. There is absolutely no use in setting an apple orchard, expecting it to take care of itself, "just growing," like Topsy, as numerous dilapidated and broken down orchards bear ample testimony. If orchards are to be cropped this must be judiciously done with the trees primarily in mind.

The best crops to grow in a young apple orchard are those requiring cultivation, or which permit the cultivation of the land early in the season. Field beans, potatoes, and garden truck of all kinds, as small vegetables, melons, etc., are among the very best crops to grow in the young orchard. Corn will do if it does not shade the trees too much. Small grain and grass should not be used, especially where they come up close to the trees. These crops form too stiff a sod and use up too much moisture. A mulch of straw, cut grass, or coarse manure will help to correct this condition somewhat when these crops must be used. After cultivation until midsummer buckwheat makes a satisfactory orchard crop in some cases.

A regular rotation may be used in the young orchard to advantage when a space is left next the trees to receive cultivation. This space should be at least two feet on each side of the tree the first year and should be widened each year as the tree grows older and larger, to four, six, and eight feet. This method has been used by the author very successfully for a number of years. Some good rotations to use in a growing orchard are: (1) Wheat or rye one year, clover one year, beans or potatoes one year; (2) oats one year, clover one year, potatoes one year; (3) beans one year, rye plowed under in spring, followed by any cultivated crop one or two years. The essentials of a good rotation for an orchard are: A humus and fertility supplying crop, preferably clover, in the north, and cow peas in the south, and at least two crops in four requiring cultivation up to the middle of the summer.

Most of the points regarding the management of young trees have already been mentioned, but a few others should have attention directed to them. Fall planted trees should not be cut back until spring. In the spring all newly planted trees should have their tops cut back rather severely to correspond with the injury to the roots in transplanting, thus preserving the balance between root and top. This will usually be about half to two-thirds the previous season's growth. From three to five well distributed branches should be left with which to form the top. During the first few years of their lives the young apple trees will need little or no pruning, except to shape them and remove crossing or interfering branches.

Constant cultivation at frequent intervals until midsummer should be the rule with young growing trees, with which this is even more important than with older trees. It is a good plan to plow the orchard in fall where possible, always turning the furrows toward the trees, leaving the dead furrows as drainage ditches between the rows. At Beechwood Farm we have always banked the trees with earth in the fall, using a shovel. This not only firms the soil about the tree, holding it straight and strong through the winter, but it affords good protection against rodents, especially mice. Where rabbits are prevalent it is well to place a fine mesh wire netting around the trees in addition to this.

CHAPTER IV
PRUNING THE TREES

Pruning is not an entirely artificial operation as one might at first thought suppose. It is one of nature's most common processes. Nature accomplishes this result through the principle of competition, by starting many more trees on a given area than can possibly survive. In the same way there is a surplus of buds and branches on each individual tree. It is only by the crowding out and the perishing of many buds, branches, and trees that others are enabled to reach maturity and fulfill their purpose. This being too slow and too expensive a process for him, man accomplishes in a day with the knife and saw what nature is years in doing by crowding, shading, and competition. Proper pruning is really an improvement on nature's method.

Neither is it true, as some claim, that pruning is a devitalizing process. On the contrary it is often stimulating and may actually increase the vigor of a weak or declining tree. All practical experience teaches us that pruning is a reasonable, necessary, and advantageous process. True, it is often overdone, and improperly done. As in many other things, certain fundamental principles underlie and should govern practice. When these are known and observed, pruning becomes a more simple matter.

Heavy pruning during the dormant or winter season stimulates the growth and tends to increase the production of wood. In the same way pruning during the summer or growing season stimulates the growth and tends to induce fruitfulness, if the tree remains healthy. But this fruitfulness is apt to be at the expense of the vigor of the tree. On the other hand, the pruning of the roots of a tree tends to check the growth of wood, the same as poor feeding. As above noted heading back a tree when dormant tends to stimulate it to a more vigorous growth.

The habit of growth of a variety has much to do with its pruning. Some varieties of apples are upright, others are spreading growers. Climate and locality greatly affect these habits of growth. So also the habit of a young tree often differs from the habit of the same tree in old age. The tendency is for a tree to continue its growth from its uppermost or terminal buds. Although the heading in of new growth checks this upward tendency and throws the energy of the tree into the development of lateral and dormant buds, nevertheless the pruned tree soon resumes its natural upward growing habit.

Plant food is taken up by the minute tree rootlets in solution and carried to the leaves where it is elaborated and then returned for use to the growing tissues of the tree. Whenever there is any obstruction above a bud the tendency is to throw the energy of the branch into a lateral bud, but if the obstruction is below the bud the branch merely thickens and growth is checked. When too heavy pruning is practiced the balance between the roots and top is disturbed. This usually results in what are commonly known as "suckers." These are caused by an abnormal condition and while they may be the result of disease or injury to the tree, they are often of great value in restoring or readjusting the proper balance between the roots and top.

Pruning a tree is a way of thinning the fruit and a good one. It may sometimes be used to influence the bearing year of trees like the Baldwin, which have an alternate bearing habit, but this is a more

theoretical than practical method. Fruit bearing is determined more by
the habitual performance of the tree than by any method of pruning,
and this is especially true of old trees. It is easier to influence
young trees. Conditions which tend to produce heavy wood growth are
unfavorable for the formation and development of fruit buds. A
quiescent state is a better condition for this.

REASONS FOR PRUNING.--With these fundamental principles in mind we
may safely outline a method of pruning an apple tree. As the desired end
is different so will the method of pruning a young tree differ from
that of an old one. There are five important things for which to prune
a young tree, namely:

1. To preserve a proper balance between the top and root at the time
of setting out. This usually means cutting off the broken and the very
long roots to a reasonable length and cutting back from one-half to
two-thirds of the growth of the previous season.

2. To make the top open in order to admit the sunlight freely. In the
humid climate of the Northeastern States, it is usually advisable to
prune a tree so as to have a rather open top. This is necessary in
order properly to color and mature the fruit.

3. To regulate the number of limbs composing the top. Probably three
branches well distributed on the trunk would make most nearly the
ideal head, but as these cannot always be obtained the best practice
is to leave from three to five branches from which to form the top.

4. To fix the branches at the proper height from the ground. This is
more or less a matter of opinion, some growers preferring a low and
others a high head. The character of the tree growth, the method of
culture, and the purpose of the tree whether temporary or permanent
greatly influence the height of the head. An upright growing variety

should be headed lower than a spreading one. Trees kept in sod or under extensive methods can well be headed lower than those under more intensive culture where it is desirable to carry on cultural operations close around them. Permanent trees should be headed higher than temporary trees. Apple trees should seldom be headed lower than a foot from the ground, nor more than four feet above it. For upright growing varieties intended as permanents, the writer prefers three to three and one-half feet and for more spreading varieties four feet; while for temporary trees eighteen inches should be a good height.

5. To do away with weak crotches and to remove crossing or interfering branches. A crotch formed by two branches of equal size, especially when the split is deep, is a weak crotch and should be avoided. Strong crotches are formed by forcing the development of lateral buds and making almost a right angle branch from the parent one. All branches which rub each other, which tend to occupy the same space with another, or which generally seem out of place, are better removed as soon as any of these tendencies are found to exist.

IDEALS IN PRUNING.--The general method of pruning the old trees and the ideal in mind for it will also influence the pruning of the young tree, especially the shaping of it. Once determined upon, the ideal should be consistently followed out in the pruning of the tree as it becomes older. As the tree comes to bearing age it will be necessary to prune somewhat differently and for other purposes. These we can conveniently consider under six heads:

1. Every tree should be pruned with a definite ideal as to size, shape, and degree of openness in mind. To have such an ideal is very important. It is only by industriously and consistently carrying it out that the ideal tree in these respects can be ever obtained. Haphazard cutting and sawing without a definite purpose in mind are really worse than no pruning at all.

2. It almost goes without saying that to remove all dead, diseased, or injured wood is a prime purpose of pruning. Dead and injured branches open the way for rot and decay of contiguous branches, and disease spreads through the tree. The removal of all such branches is as essential to the health of the tree as it is to its good appearance. In removing them the cut should be made well behind the diseased or injured part to insure the checking of rot and disease.

3. All mature apple trees should be so pruned as to keep them in the most easily manageable shape and to facilitate in every possible way the operations of tillage, spraying, and harvesting. It is most important to have the tree low enough down so that spraying and picking can be easily done. It is difficult to spray properly a tree which is more than twenty-five feet in height. Even this height necessitates a tower on the spray rig and the use of an extension pole. An apple tree should be so pruned that all the fruit can be readily picked from ladders not longer than eighteen to twenty-two feet.

Of course, if the tree has been allowed to get higher than this under previous management, sometimes we have to make the best of a bad situation. If the trees are too high head them back by cutting off the leaders, but it is not always wise to lower all trees to twenty-two feet. Heading back of old trees will be more fully discussed in the chapter on "Renovating Old Orchards." Ladders longer than twenty-two feet are heavy and clumsy to handle.

If cultivation is to be carried on close up under the tree the lower limbs must be pruned so as to allow this. It is not necessary, however, to drive a team closer than twelve or fifteen feet from a mature tree, contrary to the common belief and practice. Cultivation is least important in the first few feet of space around a mature tree. By the use of set-over tools, all that is necessary can be well cultivated without crowding the team under or against the branches.

4. As has been pointed out in the discussion of the pruning of young trees, in humid regions where the sunlight is none too abundant through the growing season, the open head is most desirable. Sunlight on the leaves as well as on the fruit is essential to good color of the fruit, and good color is a very important factor in the flavor and attractive appearance of the fruit. An open center with upright growing leaders removed gives the greatest opportunity for sunlight to penetrate through the tree.

5. As we have seen, pruning in the dormant season tends to increase the vigor of the tree. Thus winter pruning serves to secure a normal and vigorous wood growth, which is most essential to a healthy fruit-bearing tree. On the other hand, such pruning may be excessive and produce wood growth at the expense of fruit buds, throwing the tree out of bearing.

6. The sixth and last reason for pruning is to regulate the number and distribution of the wood and the fruit bearing buds. The proper balance between these is greatly affected by pruning and can be best regulated by experience with the particular tree or variety. A perfect balance is hard to get, but with study and skill it can be closely approximated. Pruning, too, may thin the fruit, as removing branches removes fruit buds. This is best done by removing small branches near the ends of larger ones. It is a much cheaper method of thinning than picking off individual fruits, but not as effective.

TIME OF PRUNING.--The particular time of the year for pruning is not vital. As between summer and winter pruning, winter is to be preferred because of the physical effect on the tree. Summer pruning is an unnatural process and should only be practiced as a last resort to check growth or induce fruitfulness, as it may result in injury to the tree. It is essential that a tree mature its foliage, which it frequently does not do after summer pruning. Diseased, dead, or injured wood should be removed when first observed, summer or winter.

Spring is the logical and usually the most convenient time to prune on the general farm. While dormant season pruning may be done at any time between November 1st and June 1st, the cuts heal more rapidly in the spring when the sap begins to flow. In regions subject to severe and drying winds in the winter, pruning should be deferred at least to late winter. Considered from every standpoint, March and April are quite the best months in which to prune. After the removal of useless branches, the normal amount of food material is delivered to fewer buds under greater sap pressure and the remaining buds are made more strong and vigorous.

In removing small branches with a knife or other cutting tool, the cut should be made upward from below and opposite a bud. On upright growing varieties the last bud left should be an outside one to induce the tree to spread as much as possible, while on spreading trees leaving as the last bud an inside one has a tendency to make the tree grow more upright. Always cut close to the parent branch, never leaving a stub no matter how young or old the tree.

Cuts of lateral branches should be made just at the shoulder of the branch where it joins the parent. A cut behind the shoulder will not heal, neither will one too far ahead of it. A stub left on a trunk or large branch does not heal, but soon begins to rot at the end where the heartwood is exposed. This gradually works back into the main branch and the tree finally becomes "rotten at the heart." All that is needed to complete the destruction is a heavy wind, an ice or a snow storm, or a heavy load of fruit.

All wounds more than two inches in diameter should be painted either with a heavy lead paint, which is preferable, or with some gas tar preparation. These things do not in themselves heal a cut, but they keep out the decaying elements, air and moisture, thus helping to preserve the branch and by protecting it to promote healing in nature's way. A little lamp black will serve to deaden the color of the paint.

PRUNING TOOLS.--The best tool to use in pruning is one which brings you nearest to your work and over which you have the greatest control to make all kinds of cuts. In the writer's experience no tool does this so smoothly and conveniently as a properly shaped saw. A good saw should be quite rigid, rather heavy at the butt, where its depth should be about six inches, tapering down to about two inches at the point. It should have a full, firm grip, be not more than thirty inches long, and should always be kept sharp. Two-edged saws should not be used because of the injury done to the tree when sawing in crotches.

Cutting shears are often very useful, especially the smaller, one-handed type which is almost indispensable in pruning young trees. The larger, two-handed shears are useful in thinning out the ends of branches or in heading back new growth. They should not be too heavy, as they are tiresome to use. The extension handled types are too cumbersome, too slow to work with, and the operator is of necessity too far away from his work for the best results.

FRUIT THINNING.--A matter which is quite nearly related to pruning is thinning the fruit, and may properly be treated here. That this is not as common a practice with most fruit-growers as it should be, the great lack of uniformity in our ordinary market apples is ample evidence. Many persons will at once raise the question as to whether or not it is practicable to thin the fruit on large apple trees. The answer is that many growers find it not only practicable, but most profitable to do so. Wherever fruit of a uniform size and color is desired, thinning is a practical necessity, especially when the crop of fruit is heavy.

The proper time to thin the fruit is just after what is commonly known as the "June drop," i.e., the falling off of those fruits not well enough pollinated or set to hold on to maturity. In thinning the fruit should be taken off until they are not closer than from four to six inches apart on the same branch, although the distance apart on any branch will depend somewhat on the amount of the crop on other parts of the tree. Never leave clusters of fruit on any branches, as some of them are sure to be small and out of shape. Furthermore two apples lying together afford a fine place for worms to get from one apple to another and they seldom fail to improve the opportunity. Step ladders and ordinary rung ladders are used to get at the fruit for thinning. The cost of the operation is not nearly as large as might appear at first thought and in practically all cases is a paying investment.

CHAPTER V
CULTIVATION AND COVER CROPPING

In its broad sense cultivation is the treatment of the soil. Thus understood orchard cultivation includes the sod mulch system as well as the stirring of the soil with various implements. In its more common and restricted meaning, however, cultivation is the stirring of the soil about plants to encourage growth and productivity. To have the apple tree in sod was once the commonly accepted method of orchard treatment--a method of neglect and of "letting well enough alone." With the advent of more scientific apple culture the stirring of the soil has come to be the more popular method. But within the last few years an improved modification of the old sod method, known as the sod "mulch" system, has attracted much attention because of the success with which a few men have practiced it. For a correct understanding of these practices and of the relative desirability of these systems we must again turn to underlying principles and purposes.

It may be said on first thought that tillage is a practice contrary to nature. But it accomplishes what nature does in another way. Tillage has been practiced on other crops than trees for so long that we think of it almost as a custom. There are, however, scientific and practical reasons for tillage.

THE EFFECTS OF TILLAGE on the soil are three fold, physical, chemical, and increasing of water holding capacity. Tillage affects the soil physically by fining and deepening it, thus increasing the feeding area of roots, and by bringing about the more free admission of air warms and dries the soil, thus reducing extremes of temperature and moisture. Chemical activities are augmented by tillage in setting free plant food, promoting nutrification, hastening the decomposition of organic matter, and the extending of these agencies to greater depth. Tillage conserves moisture by increasing the water holding capacity of the soil and by checking evaporation.

Of all these things which tillage accomplishes in a soil, two should be especially emphasized for the apple orchard, namely, soil moisture and soil texture. That moisture is a very important consideration in the apple orchard the effects of our frequent droughts are ample evidence. The amount of rainfall in the Eastern States when it is properly distributed is fully sufficient for the needs of an apple tree. By enlarging the reservoir or water holding capacity of the soil and by preventing the loss of water by evaporation, an excess of rainfall in the spring may be held for later distribution and use.

As a rule, the improvement of a poor soil texture is as effective as the supplying of plant food and much cheaper. The latter is of no consequence unless the plant can use it. Scientists tell us that there is an abundance of plant food in most soils. The problem is to make it available. Plant food must be in solution and in the form of a film moisture surrounding the smallest soil particles in order to be available to the fine plant rootlets which seek it. Good tillage supplies these conditions. Can they be obtained equally well in another way?

It is claimed by the advocates of the sod mulch system of orchard culture that it also supplies these conditions. Humus or decayed vegetable matter holds moisture. Grass or other mulch decaying in the soil increases its humus content and hence its water holding capacity.

By forming a mulch over the soil evaporation may be checked to some extent, although probably not as effectively in a practical way, as by cultivation. If there is a good grass sod in the orchard, moisture and plant food made available by that moisture are utilized, and if the grass is allowed to go back into the soil it continues to furnish these elements to the tree. But there is a rapid evaporation of moisture from the surface of the leaves of grass. In fact, grass may well serve to remove an excess of moisture in wet seasons, or from wet lands.

Laying aside theoretical considerations, let us see what practical experience teaches on this subject. We have the accurate data on a large number of western New York orchards showing the results of cultivation and other methods of soil management. These data are overwhelmingly in the favor of cultivation. In Wayne County the average yield of orchards tilled for five years or more was 271 bushels per acre, as compared with 200 bushels per acre for those in sod five years or more but otherwise well cared for,--an increase of thirty-five per cent. in favor of good tillage. In Orleans County, under the same conditions, the increase in yield due to cultivation was forty-five per cent. and in Niagara County it was twenty-two per cent. Records were made on hundreds of orchards and the results should be given great weight in determining the system to be practiced, as intelligent consideration of trustworthy records is to be encouraged.

These results were obtained in one region under its conditions and it is quite possible, although not probable, that other conditions might give different results. There are, however, special conditions as will be pointed out later, under which the sod mulch method might be more advisable than tillage. It is cheaper, makes a cleaner cover for the drop fruit, avoids the damage from tillage implements to which tilled trees are liable, and can be practiced on lands too steep to till. It often happens, too, that it fits into the scheme of management on a general farm better than the more intensive and specialized system of cultivation. And it must be remembered that we are dealing with this question from the point of view of the home farm rather than of the commercial orchardist. So that where the sod mulch gives equally good results it would be preferred under these conditions.

LATE FALL AND EARLY SPRING PLOWING.--The common tillage practice in the sections where it is most followed is to plow either in late fall or as early as possible in the spring. Whether fall or spring plowing is best depends on two things: the character of the soil and convenience. On heavy clay soils where drainage is poor it is not advisable to plow in the fall as the soil is apt to puddle and then to bake when it dries, making it hard to handle. On gravel loams, medium loams, and all well drained soils which are fairly open in texture either fall or spring plowing is practiced depending on which period affords the most time.

On the general farm where there are several crops for which the land must be prepared in spring, it would seem best to get as much of the plowing as possible done in the fall. But a large crop of apples or a large and late corn husking or potato digging may interfere with this on some farms and make spring plowing more desirable. Always plan this work in connection with the other farm work so as to give the best distribution of labor.

After fall plowing either the spring-tooth harrow or the disk harrow is best to use to work up the soil and no time should be lost in getting at this as soon as the land is dry enough in the spring. Sometimes the disk harrow can be used to work up the soil in the orchard in the spring without any plowing at all, especially on loose loams where there are few stones. But on newly plowed land a disk cuts too deep and there is too great danger of injuring the roots. On spring plowed land the spring-tooth harrow usually gives the best results. After the soil is thoroughly fined and worked into a mellow bed and as soon as the period of excessive moisture in spring is passed, a lighter implement like the smoothing harrow or a light shallow digging cultivator should be used to stir the surface of the soil only.

The growing period for an apple tree begins as early as growth starts in the spring and continues up to about midsummer. If cultivation is to stimulate growth as much as possible, it should be done during this period. The first object of cultivation in the early spring is to loosen up, aerate, and dry out the soil, which is usually too wet at that time. As cultivation is continued the soil will become fined and firmed again by the time drier weather comes on. A fairly deep digging and lump crushing tool is the best implement to use up to this time, and a disk or spring-tooth harrow meets these requirements.

After this period is passed and during drier weather, cultivation is carried on for a different purpose, namely, to conserve moisture by making a thin dust mulch of soil over the surface. This is best accomplished by shallow-going implements of which the spike-tooth harrow, the acme harrow, or a light wheel cultivator are best. As the season and the amount of rainfall vary, so must tillage operations be varied. In an early dry season begin with the lighter implements earlier. In a late wet season keep the digging tools at work later. As soon as the soil is in good physical condition the principal object of tillage is to modify moisture conditions.

As a matter of practice three to four harrowings at intervals of a week to ten days are necessary. Sometimes more, sometimes less are required, according to the character and condition of the soil and the season. The later moisture-conserving tillage should also be carried on every week or ten days, according to weather conditions. It is good practice to stir the soil after every heavy or moderately heavy rain.

Use the smoothing tools after light to medium rains and the heavier tools after packing or beating rains. In practice from five to eight or ten of these cultivations are necessary. The drier the season the more necessary does frequent cultivation become.

A COVER CROP is so closely associated with tillage that it is usually considered a part of the system. It should be sown in midsummer as soon as tillage ceases. This time will vary from July first to August fifteenth, depending on the locality, the rainfall, the crop of fruit on the trees, and on how favorable the conditions for securing a good stand of the cover crop are. The farther south the locality, or the earlier the fruit, the sooner the crop should be sown. Absence of sufficient rainfall necessitates a continuation of the cultivation, both because it is necessary to conserve all the moisture possible and because it is difficult to get a good stand of a cover crop--especially of one having small seeds--at a dry time in midsummer.

In a year when there is a full crop of fruit on the trees cultivation should be continued as late as possible as all the stimulus that can thus be secured will be necessary to help the fruit attain good size and maturity, and at the same time enable the tree properly to mature its fruit and leaf buds for the following year. On the other hand, in a year when there is not a full crop of fruit cultivation should be stopped early so as to avoid forcing a too rank growth of wood and foliage and continuing the growth of the next season's buds so late that they may not mature and therefore may be in danger of winter killing.

The different kinds of cover crops which may be used in the apple orchard will be considered in the next chapter as they are so closely associated with fertilization. Strictly speaking, however, a cover crop is used principally to secure its mulching and physical effects on the soil in the intervals between the seasons of tillage. In addition to its physical and feeding effects the cover crop serves to check the growth of trees in the latter part of the season by taking up the nitrates and a part of the moisture, thus helping to ripen the wood.

SOD MULCH.--The ordinary sod culture which is practiced in so many orchards should not be confused with the sod mulch system. The one is a system of neglect, the other of intention. In the sod mulch system the grass sod is stimulated and encouraged and when the grass dies or is cut, it is left on the ground to decay, forming a soil mulch meanwhile. The removal of grass from the orchard as hay is poor practice and should be discouraged. The grass mulch may well be supplemented by the addition of other grass, straw, leaves, coarse manure, or other similar materials. Sometimes this mulch is put on to the depth of six inches or even a foot around the tree. Thus practiced it is very effective in conserving moisture and in adding the humus which is so necessary to the soil.

Sod and tillage have somewhat different effects on the tree and on the fruit. Let us see what these effects are. It is common knowledge that fruit is more highly colored when grown in sod than when grown under a tillage system. This is probably largely due to the fact that tillage keeps the fruit growing so late that it does not mature so well or so early. Fruit is usually two or three weeks later in tilled than in sod orchards. It has been shown that fruit grown under tillage keeps from two to four weeks longer than that grown in sod. It is claimed also--but this is a disputed point--that tilled fruit has a better quality and flavor. Certain it is that fruit grown in sod is drier and less crisp and juicy.

The effect of tillage on the trees is more marked and better known. Tilled trees have a darker, richer green foliage, indicating a better and more vigorous health. The leaves are also larger and more numerous. They come out three or four days earlier in the spring and stay on the trees two weeks later in the fall than the leaves on trees kept in sod. Tilled trees make nearly twice the growth in a season that those in sod do, in fact there is danger of their making wood growth at the expense of fruit buds. Tillage also gives a deeper, better distributed root system.

Despite the advantages and the disadvantages of each system, there are times, places, and circumstances under which one is more advisable than the other. On lands rich in humus and in plant food and level so as to be easily tillable, cultivation is without doubt the best system. But it should be practiced in connection with cover crops, and the orchard should be given occasional periods of rest in sod--say one year in from three to five.

The sod mulch system of orchard culture is probably better adapted to rather wet good grass land and where mulching material is cheap and readily available. It is undoubtedly at its best on lands too steep or rough to till, or otherwise unsuitable to cultivation. Tillage is the more intensive method and where labor is scarce and high sod culture might be more advisable for this reason, other conditions being not too unfavorable.

In order to illustrate a method of management under the tillage system we may suggest the following as a good one for level to gently rolling land:

1912. Early plowing in spring, cultivation to July first to fifteenth. Then sow red clover as a cover crop.

1913. Repeat previous year's treatment, varying the time of sowing cover crop according to conditions.

1914. Let the clover grow, mowing and leaving on the ground as a mulch, June fifteenth to twentieth, and again in August.

1915. Plow early in spring, cultivate to midsummer, and then sow rye or buckwheat as a cover crop July fifteenth to August fifteenth.

1916. Repeat 1915 treatment and if trees are not growing too fast, sow clover or hairy vetch as a cover crop.

1917. Same as 1912, etc.

PASTURING THE ORCHARD.--The sod mulch system explains itself and does
not need illustration. Sod orchards are often managed as pasture for animals, however, and this practice should be discussed. An orchard is considered as pastured when a considerable number of animals are turned into it for a greater or less portion of the year. Results in orchards where pasturage has been thoroughly tried out show that it is never advisable to pasture an orchard with horses or cattle, but that fairly good results may be expected where sheep or hogs are used.

The evidence of yield of fruit and appearance of trees both indicate, that pasturing an orchard with horses or cattle is about the worst possible practice. These animals rub against the trees, break the branches, browse the limbs and leaves, and destroy the fruit as high as they can reach. All experience is against this practice which cannot be too strongly deprecated.

Pasturing an orchard with sheep, although a somewhat doubtful practice, often gives good results. Sheep crop the grass close to the ground and to some extent prevent the extensive evaporation which usually takes place from the leaves of grass. Their well distributed

manure is worth considerable. They also browse the branches to some
extent and should not be allowed to run in the orchard late in the
season as they will destroy considerable fruit.

Pasturing an orchard with swine gives better results than any other
pasture treatment of the orchard. Hogs do considerable rooting which
prevents the formation of a stiff sod and itself may often amount
almost to cultivation in well stocked orchards. A good deal of manure
is added to the soil, especially when the hogs are fed outside the
orchard. Hogs also destroy many insects by eating the wormy fruit.

Pasturage of orchards has its advantages. It gives a double
utilization of the land. It is a cheap method of management. When the
animals are fed outside the orchard, as should always be the case, it
adds considerable plant food to the soil. When plenty of outside food
can be given and when the orchard is not overstocked--the animals
should never be hungry--hogs and sheep may be used to advantage in
pasturing orchards. In very rough fields incapable of tillage, this is
undoubtedly the very best system of orchard management.

Pasturage has the disadvantage of exposing young trees to injury from
the animals, but this may be at least partly avoided by protecting
them with stakes or a heavy wire meshed screen. Hogs especially soil
the fruit and make the land rough and difficult to drive over. Under
the proper conditions pasturage may be practiced to advantage,
especially on small areas and on the general farm where it is more
advantageous than it would be commercially.

CHAPTER VI
MANURING AND FERTILIZING

Cover crops may be said to be supplementary to tillage. In the previous chapter this function has been discussed. It now remains to point out another important function--that of a green manure crop adding humus and plant food to the soil. Not only do some cover crops add plant food and all humus to the soil, but they tend to conserve these by preventing leaching, especially of nitrates, and they help to render plant food more available by reworking it and leaving it in a form more available for the tree. They sometimes act as a protection against winter injury by holding snow and by their own bulk. They also help to dry out the soil in spring, thus making the land tillable earlier.

There are two great classes of cover or green manure crops, leguminous and non-leguminous. A non-leguminous crop merely adds humus and improves the physical condition of the soil. In itself it adds no plant food, although it may take up, utilize, and leave behind plant food in a more available form for the tree's use. But in addition to these benefits, leguminous crops actually add to the soil plant food in the form of nitrogen which they have the ability to assimilate from the air by means of bacterial organisms on their roots.

NON-LEGUMINOUS CROPS.--The most important of the non-leguminous crops

are rye, buckwheat, turnips or rape, barley, oats, and millet. The
first mentioned are the most commonly used. Also in order of
importance the following are the usual leguminous cover and green
manure crops to be used: clovers, winter vetch, soy beans, alfalfa,
cow peas (first in the South). In order to determine the relative
advisability of the use of these various crops let us now look at some
of their characteristics and requirements.

Rye is one of the best non-leguminous cover crops, especially in the
young orchard, as it does not grow as well in shade as in the open. A
particularly strong point about rye is that it grows rapidly quite
late in the fall and starts early in the spring. Starting earlier than
most crops in the spring, it makes a considerable amount of growth
before the land is fit to plow. Especially in warmer climates rye
should not be sown too early in the fall--not usually before September
1st--because of this too heavy growth. Rye is also adapted to a great
variety of soils and hence will often grow where other crops will not
do well. About two bushels of seed are required per acre.

Buckwheat is probably about equally as good as rye for an orchard
cover crop, although it does not produce quite as much organic matter.
It will germinate at almost any season of the year even if it is very
dry. It is a great soil improver because of its ability to feed and
thrive on soils too poor for other crops, due to its numerous shallow
feeding rootlets. It grows rapidly and covers the ground well, but
like rye does not thrive as well in shade. Buckwheat should not be
used to excess on the heavier types of soil as it is rather hard on
the land. One bushel of seed to an acre makes a good seeding.

Turnips or rape often make good pioneer cover or green manure crops.
They are great soil improvement crops and it is comparatively easy to
secure a good stand of them even in dry weather. Sown in late July in
the North they will produce a great bulk of humus and add much

moisture to the soil, especially if they cover the ground well. Their broad, abundant leaves and high tops also hold the snow well in winter. Cow Horn is the best variety of turnips to use, as it is a large, rank grower. Use one to two pounds of seed to the acre. Rape makes an excellent pasture crop in an orchard both for sheep and hogs, but especially for the former. Eight or nine pounds of seed are necessary to the acre.

Barley, oats, and millet are not as good crops as the foregoing, because, with the possible exception of millet, they make their best growth early in the season. Moreover they take up too much moisture from the soil at a time when the tree most needs this moisture. In fact they are sometimes used for this specific purpose on wet land in too wet seasons. Two to two and one half bushels of oats or barley and one to one and one half bushels of millet to the acre are necessary for a good seeding.

Although weeds can hardly be classified as cover crops, they are often valuable ones. They grow rapidly and rank, making a large bulk of humus, without the expense of seeding. If they are not allowed to go to seed so as to scatter the seed about the farm, they often make the best of cover crops. This necessitates a mowing in September. Weeds are plants out of place, and when these plants are in place they are not necessarily weeds, as they have then become serviceable.

LEGUMES.--In general, legumes are more valuable as cover and green manure crops than non-leguminous plants, because as a rule they are more rank growers and more deeply rooted, as well as because they add nitrogen to the soil. But it is rather more difficult to secure a good stand of most legumes than it is of the crops previously mentioned for several reasons. As a rule the seeds are smaller and a large seed usually has greater germinating power than a small one. This often means much at the time of the year when the cover crop is sown. Then legumes are more difficult to grow, requiring better soil conditions. Still these should be present in good orchard soils. Drainage must be good, the soil must be at least average in fertility and physical condition, it must not be sour--hence it is often necessary to use lime--and soils frequently require inoculation before they will grow legumes satisfactorily.

Where the clovers grow well they make excellent cover crops as well as green manure crops. The chief difficulty with them is that of obtaining a good stand in a dry midsummer. The mammoth red and the medium red clovers are probably the best of their genus on the heavier soils, while crimson clover is best on sandy soils and where it will grow, on the lighter gravel loams. The latter is especially well adapted to building up run down sandy soils. Although it is somewhat easier to secure a stand of this clover, alsike does not grow rank enough to make a good cover or green manure crop. Most clovers are deep rooted plants and therefore great soil improvers physically as well as being great nitrogen gatherers. The amounts of seed required per acre for the different kinds are about as follows: mammoth fifteen to twenty pounds; red (medium) twelve to fifteen pounds; crimson twelve to fifteen pounds; and alsike ten to twelve pounds.

Where it can be readily and successfully grown alfalfa is really a better cover and green manure crop than the clovers. It is deeper rooted, makes a better top growth, and therefore adds more nitrogen and more humus to the soil than the clovers. It cannot be recommended for common use, however, as it is so difficult to grow except under favorable conditions. It requires a more fertile soil than clover, a soil with little or no acidity, good drainage, and usually the soil must be inoculated. Only where these conditions prevail can alfalfa be generally recommended.

Vetch is an excellent cover and green manure crop, forming a thick, close mat of herbage which makes a good cover for the soil. It is very quick to start growing and a rapid grower in the spring. It also adds larger quantities of nitrogen. The hairy or winter vetch lives through the hard freezing winters. Summer vetch, although an equally good grower, is killed by freezing. One bushel of seed is required per acre and the seed is expensive, which is the greatest objection to the use of this excellent crop.

Two other less well known and used leguminous crops are well worth trial as cover crops--soy beans in the North and cow peas in the South. Both are great nitrogen gatherers and as they are rank and rapid growers add large quantities of humus to the soil. Under favorable conditions they will cover the ground with a perfect mat of vegetation in a very short time. Being larger seeded, it is considerably easier to obtain a stand on dry soils and in dry seasons than it is of the smaller seeded clovers. It is usually best to sow in drills the ordinary width, seven inches, apart.

Cow peas are universally used as a cover and green manure crop in the South, but they do not thrive so well in the North. One and one half to two bushels of seed are required per acre. In the North the earlier maturing varieties of soy beans are almost equally good. One to one and one half bushels of seed are sown per acre.

Leguminous cover crops are also the best and the cheapest source of nitrogen for the apple orchard, after they are well established. Their use may be overdone, however. Too much nitrogen results in a growth of wood at the expense of fruit buds. To avoid this it is often advisable to use non-leguminous and leguminous crops alternately, when the orchard is making a satisfactory growth. Sometimes also these two kinds of crops, as buckwheat and clover for example, may be combined with good results. When this is done one half the usual amount of seed of each should be used.

EARLY PLOWING.--Many people make the common mistake of thinking that
a green manure crop must be allowed to grow until late in June in order to secure the maximum amount of growth. There are several reasons why this is not good practice. In the first place cultivation is most essential in the early spring as has been pointed out. Then moisture is better conserved by plowing under the crop early and a better physical condition of the soil secured. Plowing early in the spring warms up the soil and sets plants to work more quickly. Lastly, material rots much more quickly in the early spring when moisture is more abundant, which is very important.

An apple tree is as much a crop as anything grown on the farm and must be so regarded by those who would become successful orchardists. When it is not properly fed and cared for, good yields of fruit may not justly be expected. Especially is this true of an orchard which is being intercropped. But because of the fact that an apple tree is not an annual crop but the product of many years' growth, because its root system is deeper and more widely spread out than those of other crops, and because the amount of plant food removed in a crop of fruit is comparatively small, fertilization is less important than many persons would have us think. It is a fact that where orchards receive good cultivation and a liberal supply of humus commercial fertilizers give but medium results.

ELEMENTS OF FERTILITY.--Three elements are necessary for the growth of apple trees, nitrogen, phosphoric acid, and potash. To these lime may be added, although its benefit is indirect rather than direct as a plant food. How badly any of these elements may be needed depends on the soil, its previous treatment, and on the system of management. By learning what are the effects of these elements on the tree and fruit we may determine under what conditions, if any, their use is advisable.

Nitrogen promotes the growth of new wood and leaves, giving the latter a dark green color. In fact the color of the leaves and the amount of the wood growth are usually good indicators of the need of nitrogen. Nitrogen in excess develops over vigorous growth and prevents the maturity of wood and buds. It always has a tendency to delay the maturity of the fruit by keeping it growing late. On many varieties it tends to produce poorly colored fruits.

When trees are making a normal amount of growth in a year--say a foot to three feet or more--and when the leaves are of good size and a dark green in color, there is little need of nitrogen. But when trees are not growing satisfactorily and the leaves have a sickly yellow color, then the need of nitrogen is evident. On early soils and in long growing seasons nitrogen may be more freely and safely used than under other conditions.

The effect of phosphoric acid and potash on the tree and fruit is much more uncertain. They are supposed to influence the quality and the flavor of the fruit, giving better color and flavor, and this they undoubtedly do to some extent. Potash probably gives the leaves a darker green color. The precise effect of these two elements is at present a subject of much discussion, one set of investigators maintaining after a long and careful investigation that these effects are too small to be worth while, and the other claiming that they have a marked effect in the ways above indicated. The only safe guide is the actual local result. If the fruit is satisfactory in every way it will be of little use to try fertilizers. On the other hand, if it is not, then it will pay to experiment with them. The needs of and the results on different soils are so variable that it is always wise to experiment on a small scale before using fertilizers extensively.

STABLE MANURE.--The necessary plant food is best supplied by stable manure applied at the rate of ten loads per acre for a light application to twenty loads per acre for a heavy application. This amounts to a load for from two to five mature trees. Such an application will not only go far toward supplying the necessary nitrogen, phosphoric acid, and potash, but especially if coarse will add considerable humus and improve the physical condition of the soil.

Except on land which washes badly, manure should be applied in the fall and winter. It should not be piled near the trunk of the tree but spread uniformly over the entire surface of the ground. It is particularly important to spread the manure under and beyond the farthest extent of the branches as this is the most important feeding root area of the tree.

COMMERCIAL FERTILIZERS.--Where manure is not available or where it cannot be applied in sufficient amounts, commercial fertilizers may be resorted to, after they have been experimentally tested out. Leguminous cover crops are the best source of nitrogen, as has been indicated, but where these do not grow well, or in seasons when they have for some reason failed, nitrate of soda or dried blood are good substitutes. From two hundred to three hundred pounds of one or the other of these may be applied broadcast in the spring soon after growth is well started and all danger of its being checked by frost or cold weather is past. It is well to apply the nitrate of soda in two applications a few weeks apart, especially on soils which are leachy and in wet seasons, as part of the nitrogen may leach away if all is applied at once. These should be thoroughly worked into the soil with a spring-tooth harrow.

To supply the other two elements, from two hundred to four hundred pounds of treated rock phosphate or basic slag for the phosphoric acid, and the same amount of sulphate of potash for the potash, should be applied at any time in the early part of the season, preferably just before a light rain, and worked into the soil as before.

Home-made wood ashes are a good source of both these elements, and especially of the potash. They cannot be purchased economically in any quantity, but on the general farm there could be no better way to utilize the wood ashes made around the place than by applying them two or three bushels to a full grown tree every year or two. Wood ashes are also a good source of lime, being about one-third calcium oxide. Thus a large amount of available plant food will be supplied to the tree, and where it is needed should result not only in better wood growth but in the formation of vigorous leaf and fruit buds for the following year.

Lime is not usually considered as a fertilizer except on soils actually deficient in it. But it will usually be advisable to apply from one thousand five hundred to two thousand pounds of fresh burned lime or its equivalent, in order to correct any natural soil acidity, to hasten the decay of organic material, to increase the activity of the soil bacteria, and to improve the physical condition of the soil by floculating the soil particles and helping to break up lumpy soils. Lime also helps to liberate plant food by recombining it with certain other elements in the soil. All these effects make a more congenial medium for the leguminous crops to grow in, and it is frequently advisable to use lime for this purpose alone. After this first heavy application about 800 pounds of lime should be applied per acre every four or five years.

CHAPTER VII
INSECTS AND DISEASES AFFECTING THE APPLE

It is a common saying among farmers who have grown apples on their farms for many years that there are many more pests to fight than there used to be. How often we have heard a farmer tell of the perfect apples that grew on a certain tree "when he was a boy," before people had generally heard of codling moth, San Jose scale, apple scab, or other troubles now only too common. "We never sprayed, but the apples were fine," he says. Is this the usual glorification of the mythical past or is it true? In all probability it is a little of both, but it is undoubtedly true that insects and fungous diseases have increased rapidly of late years.

REASONS FOR PEST INCREASE.--When there is an abundance of food and conditions are otherwise favorable, any animal or plant will thrive better than when the food supply is scarce and conditions unfavorable. As long as apple trees were scattered and few in number there was not the opportunity for the development of apple pests, but as soon as they became numerous the prosperity of bugs and minute plant parasites was wonderful to see. Another factor which has been at least partly responsible for the great increase in our insect life is that man has upset nature's balance by destroying so many birds, and, by interfering with their natural surroundings, driven them away. Birds are great destroyers of insects, and their presence in the orchard should be encouraged in every possible way. Add to these facts the marvelous fecundity of the insect tribe, and the increase is less remarkable. Loss from these orchard pests has now run up into the millions. It has been estimated that the loss in the United States from wormy apples alone is over $11,000,000 annually. Thus has the necessity for fighting these enemies of good fruit arisen.

In order successfully to combat an insect or a disease it is very necessary to have a somewhat detailed knowledge of its life history and to know its most vulnerable point of attack. It is impossible to work most intelligently and effectively without this knowledge, which should include the several stages of the insect or disease, the point of attack, the time of making it, and when and with what it can be most easily destroyed. The number of insects and diseases which affect the apple is so great that it is simply out of the question to treat them all in detail here. We have therefore selected nine insects and three diseases as those pests of the apple which are most common and whose effects are usually most serious. The essential facts in their life histories and their vulnerable points will now be pointed out. The method of study may be taken as applicable to any other pests which it may be necessary to combat.

INSECT PESTS.--Of the many insects which affect either the tree or the fruit of the apple, the nine selected probably inflict the most damage and are the most difficult to control of all those in the Northeastern States. According to their method of attack all insects may be divided into two classes: biting and sucking. Biting insects are those which actually eat parts of the tree, as the leaves or fruit. These are combated by the use of stomach poisons as we shall see in the following chapter. Sucking insects are those which do not eat the tree or fruit directly, but by means of a tubelike proboscis suck the juices or sap from the limbs, leaves or fruit. Of the biting insects the five which we shall discuss are: (1) codling moth, (2) apple maggot, (3) bud moth, (4) cigar case bearer, (5) curculio. The four sucking insects discussed are: (6) San Jose scale, (7) oyster shell scale, (8) blister mite, and (9) aphis or plant louse.

1. THE CODLING MOTH, the most insidious of all apple pests, is mainly responsible for wormy apples. The adult is a night flying moth with a wing expanse of from one-half to three-quarters of an inch. The moths appear about the time the apple trees are in bloom. Each female is supposed to lay about fifty eggs which are deposited on both the leaves and fruit, but mostly on the calyx end of the young apples. The eggs hatch in about a week and the young larvae or caterpillars begin at once to gnaw their way into the core of the fruit. Three-fourths of them enter the apple through its blow end.

After twenty to thirty days of eating in the apple, during which time they become full grown and about three-quarters of an inch long, they leave the apple, usually through its side. The full grown caterpillar now secretes itself in the crevices in the bark of the tree or in rubbish beneath the tree and spins a tough but slight silken cocoon in which the pupal period is passed. This lasts about a fortnight, when the process is sometimes repeated, so that in the Eastern States there are often two broods each season.

The most vulnerable point in the career of this little animal is when it is entering the fruit. If a fine poison spray covers the surface of the fruit, and especially if it covers the calyx end of the apple inside and out, when the young larvae begin to eat they will surely be killed. It is estimated that birds destroy eighty-five per cent. of the cocoons on the bark of trees.

2. APPLE MAGGOT.--It is fortunate that the apple maggot, often called the railroad worm because of its winding tunnels all through the fruit, is not as serious a pest as the codling moth for it is much more difficult to control with a poison. A two-winged fly appears in

early summer and deposits her eggs in a puncture of the skin of the apple. In a few days the eggs hatch and the maggots begin to burrow indiscriminately through the fruit. The full grown larvae are a greenish white in color and about a quarter of an inch long. From the fruit this insect goes to the ground where the pupal stage is passed in the soil. The next summer the fly again emerges and lays its eggs.

Spraying is not effective against this insect as the poison cannot be placed where it will be eaten by the maggots. The best known remedy is to destroy the fruit which drops to the ground and for this purpose hogs in the orchard are very effective. The distribution of this insect in the orchard is limited and it has shown a marked preference for summer and autumn varieties.

3. THE BUD MOTH closely resembles the codling moth in form and size, but differs from it in color and life history. The larvae, after hibernating through the winter, appear as little brown caterpillars about May first or as soon as the buds begin to open, and a week or two later begin their work of destruction. They inflict great damage on the young leaf and fruit buds by feeding on them. When full grown the larvae, cinnamon brown in color with a shining black head, are about one-half inch long. They then roll themselves up in a tube made from a leaf or parts of leaves securely fastened together with silken threads. In this cocoon pupation, which lasts about ten days, takes place. Early in June the moths appear. There is but one brood in the North. These insects can be successfully combated with a poison spray applied early before the buds open.

4. THE CIGAR CASE BEARER winters in its case attached to a twig. When the buds begin to open in the spring it moves to them, carrying its case with it, and begins to feed on the young and tender buds. By the time the leaves are well open, it has fed a good deal on the tender buds and young leaves and is ready to make a new and larger case. This

it does by cutting a leaf to suit and then rolling it up in the form
of a cigar, whence its name. In this case the larvae continue feeding
about a month, causing much injury to the leaves, although this is not
as serious as the mutilation of the young buds in the spring, before
the tree is fully leafed out.

About the last of June pupation takes place and in about ten days the
moth emerges. The eggs are then layed along the midribs of the leaves
and hatch in about fifteen days. The newly hatched larvae become leaf
miners during August, and migrate to the branches again in the fall
where they pass the winter. These leaf and bud eating insects can be
destroyed by applying a poison to the buds before they open and again
later to the opening leaf and flower buds.

5. CURCULIO BEETLES pass the winter under leaves and grass. In the
spring they feed on the blossoms and the tender leaves. As soon as the
young fruits are formed the female deposits her eggs in a puncture
made just inside a short, crescent-shaped cut in the little apple. The
eggs soon hatch and the young grubs burrow into the fruit to the core
where they remain two or three weeks, or until full grown. The larvae
then bore their way out of the fruit and drop to the soil where they
pupate. The earliest of the beetles to emerge again feed on the fruit.
The principal damage from this pest comes from the feeding of the
beetles and the work of the larvae, although the latter is not as bad
in the apple as in the stone fruits. A poison on the young foliage as
soon as the beetles begin to feed is the best method of combating
curculio. Jarring the tree is not as practicable with the apple as it
is with the plum.

6. THE SAN JOSE SCALE, one of our worst apple tree pests, is a sucking
insect extracting the juices of the tree from the trunk, limbs or
branches, or even from the leaves and fruit when it is very abundant.
At first the growth is checked only, but as the insects develop their

work finally results in the death of the part, unless they are destroyed. The insect winters in an immature condition on the bark under a grayish, circular, somewhat convex scale about the size of a pinhead. The young, of which a great many broods are produced, are soft bodied but soon form a scale. In the early spring small two-winged insects issue from these scales.

After mating the males die, but the females continue to grow and in about a month begin the production of living young--minute, yellow, oval creatures. These young settle on the bark and push their slender beaks into the plant from which they begin to suck out the sap. In about twelve days the insects molt and in eight to ten more they change to pupae, and in from thirty-three to forty days are themselves bearing young. A single female may give birth to four hundred young in one season and there are several generations in a season. This great prolificacy is what makes the scale so serious a pest.

In fighting it every scale must be destroyed or thousands more are soon born. In order to be able to use a strong enough mixture of lime and sulphur to destroy them by smothering or choking the spray must be applied on the dormant wood in the spring or fall or both. Thoroughness is most essential.

7. THE OYSTER SHELL SCALE, although it is essentially the same in its habits and in its methods of sucking the sap from the tree is not as bad a pest as the San Jose scale because it is less prolific, there being but one brood a year. Still this scale often destroys a branch and sometimes a whole tree. The "lice" winter as eggs under the scale and hatch in late May or early June. After crawling about the bark for two or three days, the young fix their beaks into it and remain fastened there for life, sucking out the sap. By the end of the season they have matured and secreted a scaly covering under which their eggs for the next season's crop winter. A smothering spray like lime and

sulphur applied strong when the trees are dormant will practically control this scale. But the young may be destroyed in summer by a contact spray such as tobacco leaf extract or whale oil soap.

8. THE LEAF BLISTER MITE is a small, four-legged animal, so small as hardly to be visible to the naked eye. It passes the winter in the bud scales and as soon as these begin to open in the spring it passes to the tender leaves which it punctures, producing light green or reddish pimples according to the variety of apple. These later develop into galls or blisters of a blackish or reddish brown color and finally result in the destruction of the leaf. Trees are sometimes practically defoliated by this pest, and this at a time when a good foliage is most needed. Inside of the galls eggs are deposited and when the young hatch they burrow in all directions. In October the mites abandon the leaves to hibernate in the bud scales again. A strong contact spray of lime sulphur when the trees are dormant destroys the young mites while they are yet on the bud scales, which is practically the only time when they are vulnerable.

9. APHIDES, or plant lice, are of seasonal importance. Although nearly always present, it is only occasionally that they become so numerous as seriously to damage mature apple trees. But they are more often serious pests on young trees where they should be carefully watched. Their presence is determined by the curled and distorted condition of the terminal leaves on the under side of which the green or pinkish lice will be found. Eggs deposited in autumn pass the winter in this condition, hatching in the spring about the time of the beginning of the growth of vegetation. From these winter eggs females are hatched which bear living young, which may also bear living young and so on for several generations until autumn, when eggs are again deposited for the winter stage.

Fortunately weather conditions together with parasitic and predaceous insects hold them more or less in check. Because of the difficulty of getting at the underside of the curled leaves where these lice mostly work they are extremely hard to control. Lime and sulphur when the trees are dormant destroy as many of the eggs as it comes in contact with. A tobacco extract is quite effective as a contact spray in the growing season. The trees must be closely watched and if the lice appear in any considerable number they must be promptly attended to or serious damage is likely to result.

These are by no means all the insect pests which the fruit grower has to combat, but they are usually the most important. Canker worm and tent caterpillars often do great damage in unsprayed orchards, but they are easily controlled by an application of a poison as soon as they appear. The same is true of other caterpillars and leaf eating worms. Apple tree borers are frequently serious, especially in young orchards, where the trees should be regularly "grubbed" and the borers dug out or killed with a piece of wire. They may be prevented to some extent by painting the tree trunks with a heavy lime and sulphur or some gas tar preparation.

DISEASES.--Although not as numerous as insects, the diseases which attack the apple inflict great damage and are fully as difficult to control. They are caused by bacteria and by fungi which may be compared to weeds growing on or in the tree instead of the soil. If either of these works within the plant, as is sometimes the case, it must be attacked before it enters. It is very necessary to be thorough in order to control these diseases. Weather conditions influence nearly all of them materially. Of those which attack the apple tree or fruit we have selected three as the most serious and the most necessary for the grower to combat, namely, (1) apple scab, (2) New York apple tree canker, and (3) fire blight. To these should be added in the South and middle latitudes, sooty blotch and bitter rot. Baldwin spot is also frequently serious in some seasons and localities.

(1) THE APPLE SCAB, commonly known among growers as "the fungus," is the most important of our common apple diseases and is most evident on the fruit, although it attacks the leaves as well. In some seasons the fruit is made almost unsalable. This disease lives through the winter on old leaves. In the spring about blossoming time the spores are scattered by the wind and other agencies, and reaching the tender shoots germinate and enter the tissues of the plant. Their development is greatly dependent on the weather. In a season in which there is little fog or continued damp or humid weather, they may not develop at all, but where these conditions are present they frequently become very virulent.

Spraying will be governed by the weather conditions, but the mixture must be applied very promptly as soon as it is evident that it is likely to be necessary and must cover every part of the tree to be effective. The object is to prevent the spores from germinating, the spray being entirely a preventive and in no sense a cure. The disease most frequently first manifests itself on the tender new growth and on the blossoms. Two mixtures have been found to control it, namely, Bordeaux and a weak solution of lime and sulphur. One or other of these should be applied just before the blossoms open, just before they fall, and when necessary two and nine weeks later.

(2) NEW YORK APPLE TREE CANKER is usually found mainly on the trunks of old trees, but it also affects the smaller branches. Practically every old or uncared for orchard has more or less of this canker, and where it is not checked it eventually destroys the tree. This fungus is the cause of most of the dead wood found in old orchards. The surface of the canker is black and rough and covered with minute black pimples. It lives over winter and spreads from one branch or tree to another. As it most frequently enters a branch through wounds made in

pruning, these should be promptly painted over with a heavy lead and oil paint. All diseased parts should be cut out and removed as soon as observed. The value of spraying for this disease is not definitely known, but it is seldom very troublesome in well sprayed and well cared for orchards.

(3) BLIGHT appears on apple trees in three forms, as blossom blight, as twig blight, and as blight cankers. It is a bacterial disease which is distributed by flies, bees, birds, etc., and cannot be controlled by spraying. The bacteria are carried over the winter in cankers on the main limbs and bodies of the trees, oozing out in a sticky mass in the spring. These cankers should be cut out with a sharp knife cutting well into the healthy bark and then washing the wound with corrosive sublimate, one part to one thousand of water. Cutting out and destroying are also the chief remedies to be used when the blight appears in the twigs and blossoms. It is not usually as serious on apples as on pears. Some varieties, like Alexander, are more subject to it than others.

CHAPTER VIII
THE PRINCIPLES AND PRACTICE OF SPRAYING

The spraying of fruit trees in the United States is of comparatively recent origin, having been a general commercial practice for less than two decades. It involves the principle of applying with force and in the form of a fine rain or mist, water in which a poison or a substance which kills by contact is suspended. The first application of the principle was against chewing insects with hellebore. Pure arsenic was early used and soon led to the use of other arsenicals.

Our greatest fungicide, Bordeaux mixture, was discovered by accident in 1882 when it was found to control mildew in France. Up until about five years ago Bordeaux mixture as the fungicide and paris green as the poison were almost universally used. Within the last few years, however, there have been developed two substitutes which, although known and used to some extent for twenty years, have only recently come into such general use as practically to replace the old sprays. These are lime and sulphur as the fungicide and partial insecticide and arsenate of lead as a partial insecticide.

The necessity for and the advisability of spraying have already been pointed out. There is an increasing demand for fine fruit the supplying of which is possible only with thorough spraying. In the humid East especially the competition of more progressive sections in the West is demanding more and better spraying. There is no cure-all in this process. It does not make a tree more fruitful except as it improves its general health, but it does bring a larger percentage of the fruit to perfection. Certain knowledge is fundamental; the grower must know what he is spraying for, when and with what to combat it and how to accomplish the desired result most effectively.

Spraying is an insurance against anticipated troubles with the fruit, and the best and most successful growers are those most completely insured. It has many general advantages also. It stimulates the grower to a greater interest in his business because of the extra knowledge and skill required. It compels thoroughness. It necessitates spending money, therefore a return is looked for. To be sure, it is only one of the operations necessary to success, but it enables us to grow a quality of fruit which we could not obtain without it.

SPRAY MATERIALS are conveniently divided into two classes, insecticides and fungicides. An insecticide is a poison by which the insect is killed either directly by eating it, or indirectly by the caustic, smothering, or stifling effects resulting from closing its breathing pores. Direct poisons are used for insects which eat some part of the tree or fruit and are called stomach poisons. Sprays which kill indirectly are used for insects which suck the sap or juice from the tree or fruit and are called contact sprays. Arsenical compounds have supplanted practically all other substances used to combat external biting insects. Two stomach poisons are commonly used, namely, arsenate of lead and paris green, but the former is rapidly replacing the latter.

ARSENATE OF LEAD is prepared by mixing three parts of crystallized arsenate of soda with seven parts of crystallized white sugar (acetate) of lead in water, but it will not as a rule pay the grower to mix his own material, as arsenate of lead can be purchased in convenient commercial form at a reasonable price. The preparation on the market is a finely pulverized precipitate in two forms, one a powder and the other a paste. These are probably about equally good and are readily kept suspended in water. Less free arsenic is contained in this form than in any other compound of arsenic, making it safer to use, especially in heavy applications. Arsenate of lead may be used without danger of burning the foliage as strong as five or six pounds to fifty gallons of water, but three pounds is the usual and a sufficient amount for the control of any apple insect for which it is efficacious.

PARIS GREEN is being rapidly displaced by arsenate of lead for several reasons. It is a compound of white arsenic, copper oxide, and acetic acid. The commercial form is a crystal which in suspension settles rapidly, a serious fault. It is more soluble than arsenate of lead and hence there is greater danger of burning the foliage with it. Moreover, it costs from twenty to twenty-five cents a pound, and the arsenate of lead can be purchased for from eight to ten cents a pound.

The amount which it is safe to use in fifty gallons of water is from one-half to three-quarters of a pound. When paris green is used alone as a poison lime should be added. Both these arsenicals should be thoroughly wet up by stirring in a smaller receptacle before they are put into the spray tank, in order to get them in as complete suspension as possible. They may be used in the same mixture with Bordeaux or lime sulphur.

CONTACT SPRAYS.--Four compounds are used as contact sprays in combating sucking insects, namely, lime sulphur, soaps such as whale oil soap, kerosene emulsion, and tobacco extract. Of these lime sulphur is the most used and for winter spraying is probably the best. This preparation is made by boiling together for one hour or until they unite, twenty pounds of quick lime, fifteen pounds of flower of sulphur, and fifty gallons of water. Although the home made mixture is much cheaper than the commercial form which may be purchased on the market, many people prefer the latter because of the inconvenience and trouble of preparing the mixture, although there is nothing difficult about it.

This contact spray is used chiefly for the San Jose scale and the blister mite, and in order to control these must be applied strong on the dormant wood. The strength necessary will vary from one part of the mixture above mentioned or of the commercial preparation, to from seven to ten parts of water, according to the density test of the material, which should be around twenty-eight per cent. Beaume (a scale for measuring the density of a liquid) for home made, and thirty-two per cent. for the commercial mixture.

Any good soap is effective in destroying soft bodied insects such as plant lice. The fish oil soaps, although variable in composition, are often valuable, especially the one known in the trade as whale oil soap. This soap dissolved in water by boiling at the rate of two pounds of soap to one gallon of water, makes a good winter spray for scale but should be applied before it gets cold as it is then apt to become gelatinous. For a summer contact spray against lice, one pound of soap to seven gallons of water is strong enough to be effective. It is objectionable because of its odor and because it is disagreeable to make and handle. Lime sulphur is to be preferred as a winter spray, but the soap spray is often necessary and valuable for summer sucking insects.

Kerosene emulsion was formerly more commonly used than now against the scale and plant lice. It is a mixture of one-half pound of soap and two gallons of kerosene in one gallon of water--preferably in hot water. For dormant trees one gallon of this mixture should be diluted with six gallons of water. While this spray is effective it is no more so than lime-sulphur and is quite difficult and disagreeable to handle. As a summer spray, however, it is often necessary. Several preparations of petroleum known as the miscible oils are sometimes used. Their use is the same as that of lime-sulphur and they are not as good.

Within the last few years a tobacco concoction known as black leaf tobacco extract (nicotine sulphate) has come into quite common use. It can be purchased commercially under various brand names, and should be diluted according to its strength, but usually about one part to fifty of water. It may be made by boiling one pound of good tobacco stems in two gallons of water for one-half-hour. Objections to it are that it evaporates very quickly, although it is supposed to be non-volatile, and that it is expensive, but it is very convenient to use, can be readily mixed with other summer sprays, and is very effective against plant lice and mites.

BORDEAUX MIXTURE. Fungicides are mixtures of chemical compounds made up for the purpose of controlling plant diseases caused by a class of plant weeds known as fungi. There are three commonly well known and used fungicides, Bordeaux mixture, commercial lime sulphur, and the self-boiled lime-sulphur. The Bordeaux mixture is the best all-around fungicide known. It is a mixture of three pounds of copper sulphate (blue vitriol or bluestone) with three or more pounds of fresh burned stone lime in fifty gallons of water. The two compounds should be put together as fruit growers say "with water between," that is each should be diluted with the water separately before the two are mixed.

The best plan is to have stock mixtures of each in barrels, fifty gallon cider or vinegar barrels making good receptacles for the purpose. Place the bluestone in an old fertilizer or meal sack and suspend it about midway in the barrel of water. In a few hours it will all be dissolved and will remain in suspension for some length of time very well. If say fifty pounds of the copper sulphate are dissolved in

fifty gallons of water, each gallon of water will contain one pound of
the bluestone, which makes a very convenient way to measure it. So
also fifty pounds of fresh burned stone lime should be placed in a
barrel--in this case in the bottom of the barrel rather than in a
sack--just covered with water and allowed to slake, more water being
added as required up to fifty gallons. If too much water is added to
the lime at the first it will be "drowned" and its slaking checked.
These two stock mixtures, each gallon containing one pound of the
copper sulphate or one pound of the lime, are then mixed together.

It is well to fill the tank about half full of water, then put in the
required amount of the copper sulphate, and after stirring well add
the lime milk. It is a good plan to add an excess of lime as it
minimizes the danger of burning and aids the mixture in sticking to
the leaves well. If one is sure that he has at least as much lime, or
an excess of lime, it will not be necessary to test the mixture, but
if he is not, a simple test may be made with ferro-cyanide of
potassium, obtained at a drug store. A few drops of this mixture will
disappear if the lime is equal or in excess of the copper sulphate,
that is, it will be neutralized, but if it is not, they will remain a
bright purplish red. Bordeaux mixture is used in strengths varying
from three to five pounds each of bluestone and lime in fifty gallons
of water, but the former is usually sufficient.

LIME-SULPHUR.--The more important fungicides, the commercial lime
sulphur and the self-boiled lime-sulphur, are practically superseding
Bordeaux as a fungicide, not because they are necessarily better, but
because there is frequently much burning of the foliage and russeting
of the fruit from the use of the Bordeaux. This is unfortunate as the
latter is a rather more effective fungicide as well as more convenient
and pleasant to use. The self-boiled lime sulphur is a combination of
lime and sulphur which is boiled by the heat of the slaking lime
alone, and makes a pretty good substitute for the Bordeaux when it

injures foliage or fruit. This preparation of lime and sulphur differs from the commercial form used as a winter wash in that it is wholly a mechanical mixture and not partly chemical like the latter. It may therefore be used on the foliage in summer at a greater strength, there being only a very small percentage of sulphur in solution when the mixture is properly made.

Equal amounts of lime and sulphur are used, these being from eight to ten pounds each to fifty gallons of water. The mixture is best prepared in larger quantities so as to get heat enough from the slaking lime to produce a violent boiling for a few minutes. First, place say forty pounds of lime in a barrel and pour on just water enough to start it slaking nicely--about a gallon to each three or four pounds of lime is usually sufficient. Then add the sulphur and enough more water to slake the paste, keeping it well stirred meanwhile. The violent boiling of the lime in slaking will cook the mixture in from five to fifteen minutes, depending on the quality of the lime and how fast it is slaked. Just as soon as the violent boiling is over add enough cold water to stop all action. If this is not done, some sulphur will unite with the lime and burning may be the result.

This self-boiled mixture is entirely harmless to apple foliage and even appears to have a stimulating effect upon it. Against the apple scab, however, it is not as effective as the boiled wash, or the commercial preparations. For this disease a strength of from one to thirty to one to forty (that is about one and one-half gallons of the prepared mixture testing 31 to 33 Beaume to fifty gallons of water) of the commercial lime-sulphur is most effective.

SPRAY PUMPS.--The application of the foregoing spray mixtures is fully as important as the sprays themselves, for on the right application at the right time depends the efficacy of the spray. For this purpose a considerable amount of special machinery has been devised. Lack of space prevents us from going into much detail on this question, so we must be content with merely outlining the different types of machines and mentioning their accessories. Sprays are forced through single, double or triple acting pumps, either by hand or power. The three types of power available are traction, compressed air, and gasoline, the last being the most used. Steam power is practically obsolete.

The knapsack is the simplest type of hand pump, but it is of no practical use in the mature apple orchard. For small orchards and small trees several types of hand pumps are quite effective. The lever type of pump, where the handle is pushed from and pulled toward the operator, probably gives the most power with the least tiring effect, because it enables one to use the weight of the body to some extent. It is best not to have the pump attached to the spray barrel or tank, but set on a movable base of its own, as then it can be used for any one of a number of barrels. Such an outfit may be obtained for from twenty-five to forty dollars.

It is well to buy a standard make of pump, preferably from a nearby dealer, so that repairs may be readily secured. For all orchards up to three or four acres in size, and for larger orchards where the trees are not over twelve or fifteen feet in height, this kind of spray rig is the most practicable and advisable, when the expense is taken into consideration. This applies especially to the general farm.

The power of a traction sprayer is developed from the wheels. There is much discussion as to whether sufficient power to throw an effective spray can be supplied by this method. By accumulating considerable pressure by extra driving at the ends of the rows and then skipping every other tree in order to keep up the pressure, going over the rows twice, a very satisfactory pressure can be obtained for trees which are not too large. The argument for this type of machine, and it is especially applicable on the general farm, is that it can be used for other spraying on the farm as well as for the apple orchard, especially for potatoes and small fruits. It is a comparatively cheap type of power, particularly when it can be used for several purposes.

The compressed air gas sprayer comes next in point of simplicity and cost for a power sprayer. Its most economic use is found where orcharding is carried on extensively enough to pay to compress the air or gas right in the orchard. This is of course impracticable on the general farm. Therefore the air or gas must be purchased and shipped to the farm in steel tubes. This often causes delay at critical times and is rather expensive. Moreover, the gas is open to the objection of interfering with the lime-sulphur compound by precipitating some of the sulphur.

The gasoline engine is the most useful and popular type of power for the orchard sprayer, as well as for general use on the farm. Many makes are now so perfected that they give little or no trouble. One and a half or two horsepower are fully sufficient for spraying, but most farmers prefer from three to five horsepower in order to be able to use the engine more for other purposes. The latter power is open to objection for spraying purposes on account of its weight, as especially in early spring it is very difficult to haul so heavy a rig over the soft ground. Such an outfit is also rather expensive. Standard makes of gasoline engines of sufficient power for spraying cost from $75.00 to $150.00 according to horsepower and efficiency. For very large trees, for mature orchards, and for all orchards larger than four or five acres, the gasoline engine is the best source of power for spraying, particularly where it can be used for other purposes on the farm.

A double acting or two cylinder pump is most desirable. If there is plenty of power a triplex or three cylinder pump is still better. The requirements of a good pump are: sufficient power for the work desired of it; strong but not too heavy; fewest possible number of parts consistent with efficiency; brass parts and valves; and a good sized air chamber. A number of standard makes of pumps answer these conditions very well. Pumps should always be washed out with clean water when the operator is through with them and the metal parts coated with vaseline. Never leave water in a pump chamber or in the engine jacket in cold weather.

The ordinary hand pump and barrel give satisfactory use when placed on a wagon, unless the trees are very high. But for large orchards, high trees, and where larger tanks and power pumps are used it is desirable to have a special truck for the outfit. The front wheel should be made low so as to turn under the tank to enable the driver to make short turns around the trees. A tower is desirable where high old trees are to be sprayed. This should be substantial but as small as is consistent with the purpose so as not to catch on the limbs and make it difficult to get close up around the trees. The height of the platform must be regulated by the need and by the roughness of the ground. On steep side hills the wagon body on which the tank rests should be underslung.

In order to get as near to the work as possible get a long hose--from twenty to thirty feet according to circumstances. The best quality, three to five ply, is none too good. Hose should be three-eighths to one-half inch in diameter, one inch being too heavy. Extension rods are a practical necessity. They should be ten to twelve feet long and made of bamboo lined with brass, that is, as light as possible. Nozzles are very important in thorough and effective spraying. There is no best nozzle, nor one with which all the work can be done.

Several things should be considered in selecting a nozzle. First of all, it must be of convenient form so as not to catch in trees and so constructed that it will not clog easily. Second, for apple trees it should have good capacity and deliver as spreading a spray as possible. Third, the nature of the spray is very important. Insecticides should usually be applied with force in a comparatively coarse driving spray, but fungicides should be applied in a fine mist or fog so that they will settle on every part of the tree. Therein lies the difficulty of applying insecticides and fungicides together.

TIME OF SPRAYING.--Fortunately it is not necessary to make a separate application for each insect and disease, but they may be treated together to some extent. In most cases expediency demands that the arsenicals be used with the fungicides. Many growers are finding the most satisfactory results, however, from applying the arsenical spray separately, just after the blossoms fall, because of the physical impossibility of properly applying the two sprays--the driving and the mist spray--together. For most practical purposes on the general farm, three sprayings are necessary in order to secure clean fruit and four, sometimes five, are often advisable. These may be summarized as follows:

1. With lime-sulphur, winter strength, on the dormant wood in early spring.

2. With lime-sulphur and arsenate of lead just before the blossoms open (may sometimes be omitted).

3. With the same (or Bordeaux for scab) just after the blossoms fall.

4. With the same two or three weeks later.

5. With arsenate of lead eight or nine weeks later (may sometimes be omitted).

(In the south and middle latitudes where bitter rot and apple blotch occur two other sprayings may be necessary.)

6. With Bordeaux about eight or ten weeks after the blossoms fall.

7. Again with the same about two weeks later.

A Calendar for Spraying Apples

INSECTS	Nature of Injury	Before Leaf Buds Open	Before Flower Buds Open	After Petals Fall	In 2 to 3 Weeks	In 8 to 9 Weeks	Materials to Use
Codling Moth	Eating Worm			x	x	x	Lead Arsenate or Par. Gr.
San Jose Scale	Sucking Insect	x					Lime Sulphur
Oyster Shell Scale	Sucking Insect	x					Lime Sulphur
Blister Mite	Leaf Miner	x					Lime Sulphur
Plant Louse	Sucking Insect		when seen			Oil	Whale Soap or Tobacco
Cigar Case Bearer	Eating Insect		x	x	x		Lead Arsenate or Par. Gr.
Apple Maggot	Eating Worm	x	x		destroy fruit		Lead Arsenate or Par. Gr.

Bud Moth	Eating Worm	x	x	x			Lead Arsenate or Par. Gr.
Curculio	Eating Worm & Beetle		x	x			Lead Arsenate or Par. Gr.

=Diseases=

Apple Scab	Fungus	x	x	x	x	if necessary	Lime Sulphur or Bordeaux 3-3.50
New York Apple Tree Canker	Fungus	x?	cut out infections				Lime Sulphur
Leaf Spot	Fungus	x	x	x			Lime Sulphur
Sooty Blotch				x	x	x	Bordeaux Mixture and Lime Sulphur

CHAPTER IX
HARVESTING AND STORING

Apples are practically never allowed to ripen on the trees but are picked and shipped green. By "green" we mean not fully ripe, not ripe enough to eat out of hand. This is necessary for all fruit which is to be shipped any considerable distance or which is to be stored. Used in this sense green has no reference to color, but as a matter of fact, much of our fruit is picked too green, before it has even reached its full size and is well colored. There is no exact time at which apples must be picked, but this depends on many factors such as the variety, the distance to be shipped, the soil, the climate, and various other conditions, to say nothing of seasonal differences.

The time at which any variety should be picked in a particular section will be learned by experience. In general, apples should be left on the tree as long as possible in order to get the best size and color. When the apples begin to drop badly it is a pretty sure indication that it is time to pick. If the fruit is to be sold in the local market or for immediate consumption, it may be allowed to get riper than would otherwise be the case. With most varieties one picking is sufficient, but in the case of varieties like the Wealthy which does not ripen uniformly, or like the Twenty Ounce, which does not always color evenly, two or three pickings should be made. Two or three pickings are practically always necessary where fancy fruit is desired, in order to get the ideal size, color, and uniformity.

LADDERS.--There are two general types of picking ladders, the rung and the step ladders. For large trees the rung ladders are the best. They may be obtained in lengths to suit the height of the tree. Lengths of more than twenty-two or twenty-four feet become too heavy and clumsy to handle, even when made of pine, which is the best material as it is light and strong for its weight. In very old, high trees extension rung ladders are sometimes used. They are also useful for interior work but are heavy to handle. Rung ladders cost from ten to twenty cents a running foot. Step ladders are useful only on young and small trees. The two styles, the three (Japanese) and four legged, are both quite satisfactory where one can reach the fruit from them.

Receptacles for picking usually hold about half a bushel. Both baskets and bags are used, some preferring one and some the other, and a choice between them is merely a matter of personal preference. There is a little less liability of bruising the apples in bags than in baskets, but the latter are more convenient in some ways. Fruit should never be thrown or dropped into a basket but always handled carefully. Some varieties, as McIntosh, show almost every finger mark and literally require handling with gloves.

HANDLING.--The old custom of picking and laying on the ground in the orchard is a poor one and should not be followed, as it causes unnecessary handling and bruising. Moreover, fruit should be packed and hauled to storage as soon after picking as possible. Picking and placing directly on the packing table from which the apples are immediately packed is the best plan where it is practicable, but as the weather at picking time in the Eastern States is frequently quite uncertain, it is not always possible to follow this plan as closely as can be done in the West, where dry air and sunshine prevail. Still, wherever there is a considerable quantity of fruit and several pickers, the plan of packing directly from the table is best. Many growers pick in boxes and barrels and haul the apples to a packing shed to be packed later. Convenience and expediency must govern the general farmer who is not always at liberty to choose the best plan, often having to do as he can.

PACKING TABLES enable the grower to pack his fruit better because he can see better what he is doing, and to handle the fruit more cheaply and quickly and with less injury. They should be portable so that they can be moved about the orchard. A convenient type has one end mounted on wheels so that it can be pushed from one place to another. The top of the table should be made of two strong layers of canvas, one tacked firmly to the framework of the table with about three or four inches of dip and the other laid loosely over it. This plan provides a soft resting place for the fruit and the table can be easily cleaned off by simply throwing back the upper layer of canvas.

Three feet six inches is about the right width for the table, and the same sloping to three feet four inches at one end, is the correct height from the ground. Most packers like to have this gradual slope to one end so that the apples will naturally feed toward that end. The length may be anything up to eight or ten feet, beyond which the table becomes heavy and unmanageable.

BARRELS.--The standard apple barrel adopted by the National Apple Shippers' Association and made law in New York State has a length of stave of twenty-eight and one-half inches and a diameter of head of seventeen and one-eighth inches. The outside circumference of the bilge is sixty-four inches and the distance between the heads is twenty-six inches. It contains one hundred quarts dry measure. The staves are mostly made of elm, pine, and red gum, and the heads principally of pine with some beech and maple. In most apple growing sections barrels are made in regular cooper shops where their manufacture is a business by itself. Only the largest growers set up their own barrels. Practically all barrels are purchased "knocked down" and it costs from four to six cents each to set them up. Barrels can ordinarily be purchased for about thirty-five cents each, but the cost varies somewhat with the season and the region.

Apple packages should always present a neat, clean, and attractive appearance. Never use flour barrels, soiled or ununiform barrels of any kind. If a head cushion is used a good deal of waste from the crushing and bruising of the fruit will be saved. A head lining of plain or fringed paper also adds much to the attractiveness of the package. The wrapping of apples for barrel packing is hardly advisable. The fruit is pressed into the barrel tightly with one of two types of presses, both of which are good.

The lever press is more responsive and the pressure is more easily changed, but it is harder to operate. The screw press distributes the pressure more evenly with less injury to the fruit and is more powerful.

The steps in properly packing a barrel of apples are: First, see that the middle and closed end hoops are tight, if necessary, nailing them and clinching the nails; second, mark the head plainly with the grade and variety and the name of the packer or owner; then place the barrel on a solid floor or plank and lay in the facing papers (the face end being packed first); select the "facers," which should be the best representatives of the grade being packed, and ***no others***, and place them in two courses in regular order stems down; with a drop handle basket fill the barrel, using care not to bruise the fruit, and jarring the barrel back and forth on the plank as each basket is put into it in order to settle the fruit firmly in place; lastly, arrange a layer of apples stems up and apply the press, using a hatchet to get the head in place and to drive on and tighten the hoops.

THE BOX PACKAGE is rapidly growing in favor, especially as a carrier of fancy fruit. There is no standard box the size of which is fixed by law unless it be a box labeled a bushel. But two sizes of boxes are in common use, both probably being necessary on account of the variation in the size of different varieties. The "Standard" box is 101/2 by 111/2 by 18 inches inside measurement and contains 2,173.5 cubic inches (the lawful stricken bushel is 2,150.4 cubic inches). The "Special" box is 10 by 11 by 20 inches inside measurement and contains 2,200 cubic inches. The bulge when properly made will add about 150 cubic inches more, making the two boxes hold 2,323.5 cubic inches and 2,350 cubic inches respectively.

Spruce is the most reliable and in general the best material. Fir is sometimes used, but is likely to split. Pine is good if strong enough. The ends should be of three-quarter-inch material; the sides of three-eighth-inch, and the tops and bottoms--two pieces each--of one-quarter-inch material. There should also be two cleats each for top and bottom. The sides of the box should be nailed with four, preferably five-penny cement-coated nails, at each end. The cleats should be put neatly on each end and four nails put into them, going through into the top and bottom. Boxes commonly come "knocked down" or in the flat and are usually put together by the grower. They cost from ten to thirteen cents each in the flat.

There are several kinds of packs, depending on the size of the apples and the choice of the grower. The diagonal pack with each apple resting over the spaces between others is preferable, but on account of the size of the apples one is often forced to use the straight pack with the apples in regular right angle rows for some sizes. The offset pack, first three (or four) on one side and then on the other, is very much like the diagonal, but not much used on account of its accommodating too few apples in a box. The following table gives the packs, number of rows, number of apples in the row, box to use, and number of apples used to the box, as used at Hood River, Oregon:

Size expressed in No. apples per box	Tier	Pack	No. apples in row	No. layers in depth	Box used
45	3	3 St.	5-5	3	Standard
54	3	3 St.	6-6	3	Special
63	3	3 St.	7-7	3	Special
64	31/2	2-2 Diag.	4-4	4	Standard
72	31/2	2-2 Diag.	4-5	4	Standard
80	31/2	2-2 Diag.	5-5	4	Standard
88	31/2	2-2 Diag.	5-6	4	Standard
96	31/2	2-2 Diag.	6-6	4	Special
104	31/2	2-2 Diag.	6-7	4	Special
112	31/2	2-2 Diag.	7-7	4	Special
120	31/2	2-2 Diag.	7-8	4	Special
128	4	4 St.	8-8	4	Special
144	4	4 St.	9-9	4	Special
150	41/2	3-2 Diag.	6-6	5	Standard
163	41/2	3-2 Diag.	6-7	5	Standard
175	41/2	3-2 Diag.	7-7	5	Standard
185	41/4	3-2 Diag.	7-8	5	Special
200	41/2	3-2 Diag.	8-8	5	Special

It is good practice to wrap apples packed in boxes. For this purpose a heavy-weight tissue paper in two sizes, 8 by 10 and 10 by 10, according to the size of the apple, is used. A lining paper 18 by 24 in size and "white news" in grade is first placed in the box. Between the layers of apples a colored "tagboard" paper, size 171/4 by 11 or 20 by 93/4, according to the box used, is laid so as to make the layers come out right at the top. In packing the box is inclined toward the packer for convenience in placing the fruit. After laying in the lining paper each apple is wrapped and put in place. As an aid to picking up the thin wrapping paper a rubber "finger" is used on the forefinger. When the box is packed the layers should stand a quarter to a half inch higher in the middle than at the ends, in order to give a bulge or spring to the top and bottom which holds the fruit firmly in place without bruising.

There has been much discussion as to whether the box or the barrel is the better package for apples. This is needless, for as a matter of fact each is best for its own particular purpose. The barrel is best adapted as a package for large commercial quantities of fruit and where labor could not be had to pack apples in boxes even if the trade wanted them. The barrel permits the packing of a greater variety in size and shape than does the box, and these can be more easily and cheaply handled in packing.

On the other hand, the box is the ideal package for small amounts of fancy fruit, to be used for a family-or fruit-stand trade. It presents a neater and more fancy appearance and is a more convenient package to handle, as well as one which is more open to inspection. It already has a better reputation as a quality container than the barrel. As a fancy package for a limited private trade from the small general farm orchard with high-class varieties like the Northern Spy, McIntosh, and others there is no comparison of the box with the barrel.

STORAGE.--Car refrigeration and cold storage of fruit are comparatively modern developments. Few persons who have not been affected directly realize what a tremendous influence they have had upon the fruit, and particularly the apple industry. Apples could not be shipped any very great distance. Crops had to be marketed immediately and when they were large the markets were soon glutted and the fruit became almost valueless. The first hot spell would demoralize the trade altogether. Then later in the season the supply would become exhausted and famine would ensue where but a few weeks before there had been a feast. Under such conditions it is not surprising that the apple industry did not develop very rapidly and that apple growing was mostly confined to areas near the larger markets.

The coming of the refrigerator car extended fruit-growing over a much wider area. Refrigeration on shipboard opened up and enlarged the export trade. Cold storage warehouses lengthened the season by holding over the surplus of fruit, thus relieving fall gluts in the market and providing a winter supply of apples. These conditions created a more stable market with more uniform prices, extending the business from a side issue to one of chief importance. Marketing has become almost a business by itself, inducing the formation of growers' associations and creating a profitable occupation for large dealers and commission men. These conditions, too, have led to speculation.

Two kinds of storage are used, common or cellar storage and cold storage. Both are about equally available, but the latter is too expensive for the small grower. There is always a question as to the advisability of the small grower storing his fruit. Storage means a degree of speculation. "A bird in the hand is worth two in the bush," especially when the bird is a good one. So far as rules can be laid down, the following are pretty safe ones to keep in mind: It is safest to store apples when they are of the highest quality; in a season most unfavorable to common storage; when the fewest are being stored; when the price in the fall is medium to low, never when high; and when one can afford to lose the whole crop.

Successful storage requires several things: good fruit, stored immediately after picking, careful sorting and handling, subsequent rest, and a reasonable control of the temperature. The functions of storage are to arrest ripening, retard the development of disease, and furnish a uniform, cold temperature. Storage of apples does not remedy over-ripeness nor prevent deterioration of already diseased, bruised, or partly rotted fruit. There are three general methods of storage: (1) by ventilation, (2) by the use of ice and (3) by mechanical means.

Cooling by ventilation offers the most practical system for a farm storage. It requires that there be perfect insulation against outside temperature changes, adequate ventilation, and careful watching of temperatures. To provide for good insulation a dead air space is necessary. This can be secured by a course of good two-inch boards with one or two layers of building paper inside and out, over a framework of two-by-fours. Over the building paper tight, well matched siding should be laid also inside and out. Two of the dead air spaces will make insulation doubly sure.

To provide for proper ventilation construct an intake for cold air at the bottom, and an outlet for warm air at the top of the room. These should serve all parts of the room, one being necessary for this purpose every twelve to sixteen feet. Do not depend too much on windows. Warm-air flues should be twelve inches square and six to twelve feet long.

The attention to such a house is most important. Keep it closed tightly early in the fall with blinded windows. When nights get cool open the doors and windows to let in cold air, closing them again during the day. On hot days close the ventilators also. In this way a temperature of 36 to 40 degrees Fahr. can be secured in early fall and one of 32 to 33 degrees Fahr. later. This is probably the cheapest as well as the most practical method of farm storage.

Ice storage is quite practical in the North, but more expensive. The principle of such a storage is to keep ice above the fruit, allowing the cold air to flow down the sides of the room. A shaft in the middle of the room will serve to remove the warm air. This method is open to the objection of difficulty in storing the ice above the fruit. Moreover the uniformity of its cold air supply is questionable. Mechanical storage in which cold temperatures are secured by the compression or absorption of gases is altogether impracticable for individual growers, as it costs from $1.50 to $2.00 a barrel of capacity to construct such a storage. Rents of this kind of storage range from 10 to 25 cents a barrel per month, or 25 to 50 cents a barrel for the season of from four to six months.

CHAPTER X
MARKETS AND MARKETING

Having produced a good product, there remains the problem of making a profitable and satisfactory disposition of it. In many ways marketing is the measure of successful fruit growing. Of what use is it to prune well, cultivate well, spray thoroughly, or even pack well the finest kind of product, if after the expense of these operations is paid and the railroad and commission agents have had their share, no profit remains to the producer? Many growers find it easier to produce good fruit than to market it at a good price, and this is especially true of the general farmer. Failure to market well spells failure in the business of fruit growing. Successful marketing presupposes a knowledge of the requirements of different markets as to quality, varieties, and supply demanded in those markets. Methods of distribution are also one of the great factors in this problem of marketing.

TYPES OF MARKETS.--There are two general types of markets, the local, which is a special market and the general or wholesale market, both of which have different but definite requirements. The local market handles fruit in small quantities, but usually with a larger margin of profit per unit to the producer. As a rule delivery is direct in a local market, and thus commissions are saved. Competition is also more or less limited to one's neighbors. More varieties, including less well known ones, are called for. Appearance does not count for as much as quality, which is of first importance. Fruit may be riper as it is consumed more quickly and meets with less rough handling. Packages are usually returned to the grower. Special markets are often willing to pay extra for fruit out of season, and they always require special study and adaptation to meet their needs.

The general or wholesale market handles fruit in larger quantities, usually with a smaller margin of profit. A selling agent or commission man is the means of disposing of fruit in such a market, where competition is open to the whole country and sometimes to the world. Only standard well-known varieties find a ready and profitable sale. Great attention is paid to appearance and comparatively little to quality. Fruit shipped to a wholesale market must be packed in a standard package, which is not returned, but goes with the fruit, and must be packed so as to endure rough treatment. Out of season fruit is not in demand, but even the general market sometimes has special preferences.

Almost every market has favorite varieties for which it is willing to pay a larger price than other markets. Just as Boston wants a brown egg and New York a white one, so these and other cities have their favorite varieties of apples. Some markets prefer a red apple, others a green one, although the former is most generally popular. In the mining and manufacturing towns working people want smaller green apples, or "seconds," because they are cheaper. Many second-class hotels prefer small apples, if they are well colored, as they go farther. The fashionable restaurant and the fruit stand are the markets for large, perfect, and highly colored specimens. Housewives demand cooking apples like Greenings, hotels want a good out-of-hand apple like the McIntosh, while private families have their own special favorites. As will readily be seen, the producer's problem is to find the special market for what he grows.

It has been said that different markets have special varietal preferences, paying a better price for these than do other markets for the same quality. We can only take the space here to point out a few of these preferences. The Baldwin is by all odds our best general market and export variety. It is the workingman's apple and finds its best sale in our largest cities, particularly in New York and Chicago. The Rhode Island Greening is a better seller in the northern markets than it is in the southern, finding its best sale in Boston and in New York. The Northern Spy is highly regarded by all our large northern and eastern markets, is fairly well liked by the middle latitude markets, but not popular south of Baltimore and Pittsburgh or west of Milwaukee.

Central western markets appear to prefer the Hubbardson, but this apple is fairly good in all markets. King is well thought of nearly everywhere. Ben Davis is a favorite in the South, New Orleans especially preferring it on account of its keeping quality. Jonathan has a good reputation everywhere. Dutchess of Oldenburg is regarded as excellent in Buffalo and Chicago. Wealthy, although generally a local market apple, is well known and liked in all markets. Twenty Ounce is spoken well of nearly everywhere. The Fameuse is not well liked in the South, but popular in the North, etc. These particular facts as to varieties are best learned by experience and by observation of the market quotations.

THE COMMISSION MAN.--The present system of marketing fruit products makes the commission man almost a necessity in the general market. Neither the grower nor the local dealer can ship directly to the consumer or even to the retailer, except in a very limited way. It may be impracticable to devise any other workable system, but it must be remembered that every man who touches a barrel of apples on its journey from producer to consumer must be paid for doing so, and this pay must come either out of the seller's price or be added to the buyer's price. But so long as present conditions of marketing and distribution prevail, so long will a selling agent in the general market be necessary, and the evil cannot be ameliorated by ranting against it.

An unfortunate impression prevails that all commission men are dishonest. This is not true, although undoubtedly there are many scoundrels among them, as they have shippers almost completely at their mercy. The best method under our present system is to choose an honest commission man in the city where you sell, to get acquainted with him, to let him know that your trade will be in his hands only so long as he treats you fairly, and then supply him with as good quality of stuff as you can produce. This plan has worked out well with many successful growers and marketers.

Perhaps the greatest difficulty to be overcome in successfully finding good markets is that of proper distribution. As has been pointed out in the previous chapter, there has been a great increase in the production of apples and hence in competition, accompanied by speculation and more intensive methods in all phases of the business. A necessity has arisen for the production of the best at a minimum cost, as well as for finding the best market for that product. In the rush for the best market every seller is apt to be guided only by his own immediate interest without due regard for the fact that others are acting in the same way or that there is a future. The result is the piling up of fruit in a market of high quotations, and a subsequent drop in the price. Then all turn from such a market to a better one with the result that a famine often results where but a few weeks or even days before there had been a feast.

Thus it often happens that one market may have more fruit than it can possibly dispose of at the time, while another, perhaps equally good, goes begging. Such conditions are ruinous to trade. Growers are disappointed and ascribe the cause to the commission man. Consumers are unable many times to profit by a glut in the market but promptly blame the middleman or the grower when the supply is small and the price high.

Other difficulties with our system of marketing are non-uniformity of the grades, the packages, or the fruit itself. There should be a clear definition of just what "firsts" and "seconds" are and this definition rigidly adhered to. Transportation is too frequently insufficient, not rapid enough, especially when perishable fruit is shipped in small lots, and usually at a too high rate. There are undoubtedly too many middlemen between producer and consumer. Growers sell to local dealers who sell to wholesalers at the receiving end. These sell to wholesalers at the consuming end, who may sell to jobbers, who sell to retailers. Each man must have his profits, all of which greatly increases costs.

CO-OPERATION.--Individuals have practically no power to remedy such a state of affairs. So long as producers act independently they will have little power either to bring about favorable legislation or to better such market conditions. Acting together as a unit growers have accomplished great things which can be repeated. The co-operative principle has been well tried out in California, where it was first put into operation with citrous fruits, in several other Western States with apples, and in Michigan and the Province of Ontario.

Co-operative associations study carefully the law of supply and demand and take steps to adapt their shipments to it. They standardize the grade, the package, and the fruit, and govern their shipments to given markets by the needs and the demands of those markets. Their unity of effort enables them to make great savings in the purchase of supplies, such as packages, spraying material, fertilizers, etc., and in obtaining and distributing frequently knowledge of markets and market conditions. They also advertise their products, making them better known, creating a demand for them, and by means of correspondence or traveling agents seek out the best markets.

There are now several large fruit exchanges operating over wide sections of country. But the local associations are the vital units in any co-operative movement. Such associations should be incorporated under State laws so that they can do all sorts of business when necessary. Six simple objects should be kept in mind, namely, (1) to prevent unnecessary competition, and to supervise and control distribution of products; (2) to provide for uniformity in the grade, package, and fruit; (3) to build up a high standard of excellence and to create a demand for it; (4) to economize in buying supplies and selling products; (5) to promote education regarding all phases of the fruit business; and (6) when necessary to act as a buying and selling agent for the community.

Such an association requires a board of directors, a treasurer, and an active and well-paid manager. The latter is most important, as upon his honesty, ability, and energy will largely depend the success or failure of the organization. Sometimes where fruit is packed in a central packing house or under an association brand or guarantee, a foreman packer is also necessary. The capitalization required for such an enterprise is not necessarily large, unless warehouses or packing houses are built. These are usually better rented until the organization becomes well established.

The shares should be small so that every member may be financially well represented, and members should be prohibited from holding more than a small percentage of the total shares, in order to prevent possible monopoly. Dividends on stock held should only be expected from business done outside the association membership, interest on money invested being obtained in the handling of members' products at cost. Receipts should be given growers for just what they bring in, and they should then be paid according to the grade of fruit which they contribute, prices for the same grade being pooled. The charge to growers for handling should be actual cost, but outsiders' products should be handled at a small profit in order to induce them to come into the association. The same method should be followed in purchasing supplies.

The general result of such co-operation is that the consumer gets a better product for his money and the grower receives a better price for his product. It is very essential to the success of the organization that growers stick together, even through low prices and discouragement which so often come, until they are firmly established. Substantial reduction in the cost of the product to consumers can only come by similar co-operation among them at the buying end and by the co-operation of both consumers and producers for distribution and handling in market.

If a neighborhood does not feel yet ready to attack this problem in this thorough and businesslike way, it will be advantageous and a step in the right direction if they simply agree on certain standards of quality and packing and then pool their product for marketing. This method has also been followed with success.

CHAPTER XI
SOME HINTS ON RENOVATING OLD ORCHARDS

Nearly every general farm in the humid part of the United States has
its small, old apple orchard. For the most part these orchards were
planted in order to have a home source of supply of this popular
fruit. In fact, but few orchards have been planted on a commercial
scale with a view of selling the fruit, until recently and outside of
a few sections. Therefore, as a rule we find these old farm orchards
to consist of a few acres containing from twenty-five to two hundred
trees. These trees are usually good standard varieties which have been
the source of much apple "sass," many an apple pie, and many a barrel
of cider-vinegar.

Not having been set for profit, these trees received little care.
Orchards were cropped in the regular rotation, or with hay, or
pastured. Farmers then knew little of modern methods of orchard
management. The orchard was regarded as an incumbrance to the land,
which had to be farmed to as good advantage as possible under the
circumstances, and if the apple trees by any chance yielded a crop,
the owner regarded himself as fortunate indeed.

But conditions have now changed. Both local and foreign markets have
been opened up and developed so that the demand for good fruit is
great. It will be some time before the thousands of acres of orchards
which have been and are being planted to meet this demand will be able

to do so in any adequate way. It has been shown in Chapter I how heavy has been the falling off in the supply, even in the face of these heavy plantings. Meanwhile we must turn to the old neglected farm orchards for our supply of apples. Just at this particular time the renovation of these old orchards offers a splendid opportunity to increase the farm income.

The question is a live one on nearly every general farm in the East. Will it pay to try to renovate my old apple trees? If so, what should I do to make them profitable? What will it cost and what returns may be expected? The latter question will be taken up in the following chapter, but here we must try to indicate under what conditions it may pay to renovate an old orchard, as well as those under which it may not pay, and also how to go about the problem.

NECESSARY QUALITIES.--An apple orchard must have certain qualifications in order to make it worth while to spend the time and money necessary to accomplish the desired results. These we may take up briefly under five heads: (1) varieties, (2) age, (3) number or "stand" of trees, (4) vigor and health of the trees, and (5) soil, site, and location. The discussion of these subjects in Chapters II and III has equal application here, but we may perhaps point out their specific application more definitely in the case of the old neglected farm orchard.

(1) Varieties should be desirable sorts. If they are the best standard market varieties, as is often the case, so much the better. Otherwise little is gained by improving the tree and fruit. Poor or unknown varieties have little or no market value, except perhaps a very local one. If the trees are not too old and are fairly vigorous, poor varieties may sometimes be worked over by top grafting to better varieties. Characteristics which may make, a variety undesirable are: inferior quality; unattractiveness in color, shape, or size; lack of

hardiness in the tree or keeping quality in the fruit; low yield; or being unknown in the market with its consequent small demand. Summer varieties are worth renovating only when they are in good demand in a nearby local market.

(2) Vigor is more important than age in the tree, but is closely correlated with it. Ordinarily one should hesitate to try to renovate a tree more than forty or fifty years old, but this must always depend almost wholly on its condition and other characteristics.

(3) In order to make a business of renovation and to do thorough work which means expense, there must be enough of the orchard to justify the expenditure of the time and money. This affects the results not only in expense, but in economy in management, equipment, and marketing. There should be at least an acre of say thirty trees, and better, more than that number to justify the expense of time and money necessary for renovation. One hundred trees would certainly justify it, other conditions being favorable. Then, too, the trees should be in such shape that they can be properly treated without too great trouble and expense, i.e., not too scattered or isolated or in the midst of regular fields better adapted for other crops.

(4) Vigor and good general health are of great importance. Many old trees are too far gone with neglect, having been too long starved or having their vitality too much weakened by disease to make an effort for their rehabilitation worth while. Good vigor, even though it be dormant, is absolutely essential. Disease weakens the tree, making the expense of renovation greater. Moreover, all diseased branches must be removed, requiring severe cutting and often seriously injuring the tree. Disease too often stunts the tree to such an extent as to make stimulation practically impossible. Such matters should be carefully looked into before attempting renovation.

(5) If the soil, site, and location are all unfavorable or even if two of these are not good, time and money are likely to be wasted on renovation. What constitutes unfavorable conditions in these respects has already been pointed out in Chapter III.

Practically the same principles of pruning, cultivation, fertilization and spraying apply in the management of the old orchard as in any other orchard. It may be well, however, to restate these, briefly pointing out their special value and application to the old neglected orchard together with the few modifications of practice necessary. The steps to be taken are four: (1) pruning, (2) fertilizing, (3) cultivating, and (4) spraying.

(1) PRUNING.--Old and long-neglected apple orchards usually have a large amount of dead wood in them. This may be removed at any time of the year, but fall and winter are good times to begin the work. If the trees are high and the limbs scattered and sprawling so that the middle of the trees is not well filled out, the trees should be headed back rather severely. Such trees may safely have their highest limbs cut back from five to ten feet. It is best not to remove too many branches in one year, but to spread severe cutting back over at least two years, as so much pruning at one time weakens the tree and causes an excessive growth of "suckers." Each limb should be cut back to a rather strong and vigorous lateral branch which may then take up the growth of the upright one. The effect of such heading back will be to stimulate the branches lower down and probably to bring in more or less "suckers." The following year the best of these suckers should be selected at proper points about the tree, headed in so as to develop their lateral buds, and encouraged by the removal of all other suckers to fill in the top and center of the tree in the way desired. All such severe heading in should best be done in the early spring.

(2) FERTILIZING.--At some time during the late fall or winter twelve to fifteen loads of stable manure should be applied broadcast on each acre, scattering it well out under the ends of the branches. This will amount to a load to from three to five trees. In case manure is not available, or sometimes even supplementary to it in cases where quick results are wanted 100 to 200 pounds of nitrate of soda, 300 to 500 pounds of acid phosphate, and 150 to 200 pounds of sulphate or muriate of potash should be applied in two applications as a top dressing in spring, as soon as growth starts, and thoroughly worked into the soil. This will give the trees an abundance of available plant food, which is usually badly needed, and help to stimulate them to a vigorous growth. Such heavy feeding may easily be overdone and should be adjusted according to conditions and the needs of the orchard.

(3) CULTIVATING.--If the orchard has been in sod for a number of years, as is often the case, it is usually best to plow it in the fall about four inches deep, just deep enough to turn under the sod. By so doing a large number of roots will probably be broken, but such injury will be much more than offset by the stimulus to the trees the next season. It is a good plan to apply the stable manure on the top of this plowed ground early in the winter. Fall plowing gives a better opportunity for rotting the sod and exposes to the winter action of the elements the soil, which is usually stale and inactive after lying so long unturned. In the spring the regular treatment with springtooth and spiketooth harrows should be followed as outlined in Chapter V.

(4) SPRAYING in the old orchard is essentially the same as elsewhere. It is necessary, however, to emphasize the first spray, the dormant one, winter strength on the wood. This is the most important spray for a neglected orchard and it should be very thoroughly applied. It is a sort of cleaning-up spray for scale, fungus, and insects which winter on the bark. In orchards where the San Jose scale is bad a strong lime-sulphur spray should also be used in the late fall in order to

make doubly sure a thorough cleaning up. It is usually a pretty good plan to scrape old trees as high up as the rough, shaggy bark extends, destroying the scrapings. For this purpose an old and dull hoe does very well. This treatment will get rid of many insects by destroying them and their winter quarters.

PATCHING OLD TREES.--A few suggestions on patching up the weak places in an old tree may not be entirely out of place. The question is often asked, will it pay to fill up the decayed centers or sides of old trees? If the tree is otherwise desirable to save, it usually will. Scrape out all the dead and rotten material, cleaning down to the sound heart wood. Then fill up the cavity with a rough cement, being careful to exclude all air and finishing with a smooth, sloping surface so as to drain away all moisture. This treatment will probably prevent further decay and often acts as a substantial mechanical support.

Trees which are badly split or which have so grown that a heavy crop is likely to break them over should be braced with wires or bolts. Where the limbs are close together a bolt driven right through them with wide, strong washers at the ends is very effective in strengthening the tree. Where limbs must be braced from one side of the tree across to the other wires are the best to use. They may be fastened to bolts through the limbs with wide washers on the outside hooks on the inside, or by passing the wire around the branches. In the latter case some wide, fairly rigid material such as tin, pieces of wood, or heavy leather should be used to protect the tree from the wire which would otherwise cut into the bark and perhaps girdle the limb.

COST.--For the benefit of those who would like to get some idea of the probable cost of renovating old apple orchards, the following estimate made by the writer in a recent government publication on this subject is given. This estimate has been carefully made up from actual records kept on several New York farms. Because these costs are very variable according to the condition of the orchard, both maximum and minimum amounts are given per acre for the first year only.

	Minimum cost	Maximum cost
Plowing	$2.00	$3.00
Manure, 10 to 20 loads at $1, or their equivalent in commercial fertilizer	10.00	20.00
Hauling manure	5.00	10.00
Pruning and hauling brush	5.00	10.00
Disking or harrowing twice	1.00	1.50
Disking or harrowing 3d or 4th time	.50	1.00
Cultivating two to four times	.50	1.00
Spraying once with L.S. dilution 1 to 9--material	2.00	4.00
Spraying once, L.S., labor	1.00	1.50
Spraying second time with L.S. dilution 1 to 40, labor and material	1.50	2.50
Spraying third time with same	1.50	2.50
	------	------
Total cost	$30.00	$57.00

CHAPTER XII
THE COST OF GROWING APPLES

Two factors have always operated to deter many persons from taking up fruit growing as a business or even as a side issue on the farm, and they will probably continue to be an obstacle for more time to come. These are the comparatively large investment required and the necessarily long period of waiting before paying returns can be obtained. Farmers who have not gone into the business of fruit growing because they could not afford this heavy investment or to wait so long for returns have been wise. Others who, though lacking the necessary capital, still have planted heavily have learned to their sorrow the importance of capital in the business both for the original investment and to carry the enterprise. And yet with sufficient capital and the proper conditions there is no more attractive or profitable line of agriculture than fruit growing.

Who knows what it costs to grow an orchard to bearing age? Or what it costs to produce a barrel of apples? We venture to say that very few persons do. Because of the large investment both in fixed and in working capital it is most important to know these costs. Moreover an accurate knowledge of the financial conditions and facts in any business is of first importance to intelligent management. For these reasons every grower ought to keep careful records of the cost and income from each field or orchard every year in order to determine as accurately as possible what his crops have cost him per unit and per acre and what rate of interest he has realized on his investment. As farming becomes more intensive competition increases, costs multiply, and the margin of profit on any given unit becomes smaller. It therefore becomes increasingly necessary to have accurate records on the cost of production.

FACTORS IN THE COST OF PRODUCTION.--The value of records depends on their accuracy and on their completeness. There are a great many factors which enter into the cost of production. For convenience these may be classified as cash costs and labor costs. Labor charges should include the work of both men and teams at a rate determined by their actual cost or by a careful estimate. Man labor costs are easily reckoned, as they are either simple cash or cash plus board and certain privileges, the value of which should be estimated in cash.

The value of horse labor is more difficult to determine. It is made up of interest on valuation, depreciation, stable rental, feed, care, etc. A fair estimate of this cost is $10 a month or $120 a year for a horse. Cash costs are interest on the investment and on the equipment in machinery, etc., or rental of the same, taxes, a proper share of the general farm expenses such as insurance and repairs of buildings, telephone, etc., the cost of spraying material, packages, fertilizers, etc.

There are many ways of keeping such a record. Any method which accomplishes the result in a convenient and accurate manner is a good one. It will usually be found necessary to keep a cash account or day book, entering all items in enough detail to make possible their later distribution to the proper field or crop, and also to keep a diary of all labor. Any form of diary will answer the purpose, but one which has ruled columns at the right side of the page in which to indicate the crop or field worked upon, and the number of hours worked is more convenient and therefore more desirable.

AN EXAMPLE.--For a number of years the author has kept such records on his farm in western New York. As an illustration of the method and in order to give the reader a general idea as to what the costs above referred to are likely to be we venture to give the following tables. It must be remembered, however, that practically everyone of the above mentioned factors varies with the conditions under which the orchard is managed and that these figures are not *an* average but **one** average and on one farm. True averages are arrived at only by bringing together a large number of figures. In any case, the question of cost is essentially an individual problem on every farm. These figures are of value only as an example of the method and the cost on one farm under its own special conditions.

The orchard for which the following figures were given was set in the spring of 1903, and the records begin with that year and end with 1910, covering a period of eight years in all. Throughout this period other crops have been grown between the tree rows, thereby offsetting to a large extent the cost of growing the orchard. Forty trees at the north end of the orchard are pears, but they have received substantially the same treatment as the apples and have not affected the cost. In 1904, 211 plum trees were set as fillers one way. The apple trees were set 36 by 36 feet apart, so that, filled one way, the trees stand 18 by 36 feet apart. The orchard is ten rows wide and forty-seven long, containing in all 467 trees.

BRINGING TO BEARING AGE.--The first of the following tables is given as a sample of one year's records, that of 1907, on this orchard in order to show both the manner in which the costs were made up and what the items amounted to in one year:

FIELD A--1907. FIFTH YEAR

Operation	Total hours Man	Total hours Horse	Total cost	Hours per acre Man	Hours per acre Horse	Cost per acre	Cost per 100
Mulching	3	6	$1.05	.455	.91	$0.16	$0.22
Pruning	11	...	1.65	1.67	...	.25	.35
Cultivating 1	7	7	1.75	1.06	1.06	.26	.38
Cultivating 2	10	10	2.50	1.51	1.51	.38	.54
Cultivating 3	6	6	1.50	.91	.91	.23	.32
Plowing in fall	47	94	16.45	7.12	14.25	2.50	3.52
Banking trees	12	...	1.80	1.82	...	.27	.39
Harrowing	21	42	7.35	3.18	6.36	1.11	1.58
	---	---	------	-----	-----	-----	-----
Total lab. cost.	117	165	$34.05	17.73	25.00	$5.16	$7.30
4 loads manure at $1.50			6.00		.91		1.29
Equipment charge			1.15		.174		.25
Taxes			5.29		.801		1.13
Interest			38.48		5.83		8.23
			------		-------		------
Total cost			$84.97		$12.875		$18.20

INCOME, COST AND PROFIT ON BEANS--FIELD A--1907

Income			Cost	Profit
75 bushels at $1.50	$112.50			
31/2 tons pods at $6	21.00	$133.65	$94.50	$38.85

LOSS ON FIELD A--1907

	Total	Per acre
Net income from beans	$38.85	$5.89
Cost of orchard	84.97	12.87
	------	------
Loss	$46.12	$6.98

A summary of the cost of the orchard, the net income from the crop, the income from the orchard and the profit and loss by years for the eight years follows:

SUMMARY OF COSTS FOR EIGHT YEARS, FIELD A

Year	Crop grown	Net income from crop	Income from orchard	Cost of orchard	6.6 acres Profit	Loss
1903	Corn	$ 15.17	...	$109.87	...	$ 94.70
1904	Beans	42.57	...	216.16	...	173.59
1905	Beans	43.13	...	83.78	...	40.65
1906	Beans	120.90	...	80.14	$40.76	...
1907	Beans	38.85	...	84.97	...	46.12
1908	Corn	37.68	...	64.22	...	26.54
1909	Oats and strawberries	100.61	$27.88	84.73	43.76	...
1910	Wheat	60.70	38.65	96.35	3.00	...
		------	------	------	------	-------
Totals		$459.61	$66.53	$620.22	$87.52	$381.60

Net loss on field for eight years	$294.08
Average annual loss	38.76
Total cost an acre, exclusive of income	124.27
Total cost an acre, including income	44.55
Total net cost a hundred trees	62.97
Total net cost an apple tree	1.37

Total net cost an apple tree, exclusive of income	3.80
Total labor cost an acre	35.09
Total cash cost an acre	89.19

We find that this orchard has cost $124.27 an acre during the eight years of its life, but that the $79.72 an acre of crops grown in the orchard has brought this cost down to $44.55 an acre. It is safe to say that the orchard would have cost even more than it did had it not been for the crops, for many operations charged directly to the crops would of necessity have been charged to the trees. The cost a hundred trees does not mean much, as it often happens that not all the trees are covered by an operation and as the number of trees an acre greatly affects these costs.

We have another and younger orchard upon which a record has been kept. This orchard of five acres contains 126 standard apple trees, "filled" both ways with 375 peach trees. It was set in the spring of 1908, so that the trees have grown four seasons. The permanents (apples) are set 36 by 40 feet apart, so that, with the peaches between, the trees stand 18 by 20 feet apart. A crop of beans has been grown between the tree rows each season. The first season a full seven rows, twenty-eight inches apart, were planted in the wider space; the second and third season six rows, and the last season only four rows. The crop has been very good each year until the last. One application of manure, one crop of clover and one seeding of rye have been plowed under, and in addition a liberal amount of commercial fertilizer has been used with each crop. This year the peach trees bore their first crop. The record of the four years is as follows:

SUMMARY OF THE COST OF A FOUR-YEAR-OLD APPLE AND PEACH ORCHARD

Year	Crop grown	Net income from crop	Income from orchard	Cost of orchard	Profit	Loss
1908	Beans	$63.37	...	$130.12	...	$62.75
1909	Beans	66.70	...	$85.03	...	18.33
1910	Beans	79.81	...	83.39	...	3.58
1911	Beans	53.20	$46.05	61.95	$37.30	...
Totals		$267.08	$46.05	$360.49	$37.30	$84.66

Total cost an acre, exclusive of income	$72.10
Total cost an acre, including income	9.47
Total net cost a hundred trees	4.73
Total net cost an apple tree	.376
Total net cost an apple tree, exclusive of income	2.86

These figures show a still lower cost of growing trees to bearing age. After paying all expenses connected with the growing of the trees, including the interest on the land at $150 an acre, and deducting the net profit from the crops of beans and the sales from the first crop of peaches we find that the growing of the trees has cost us $9.47 an acre, or 371/2 cents an apple tree at four years old. Had no crop been grown in the orchard it would have cost us at least $62.89 an acre after deducting the income from the first peach crop. The peach trees are now at full bearing age, and should show a good profit from this time on. Possibly at five and certainly at six years of age this orchard will entirely have paid for itself. The only possible further charge which could be made against this orchard is the crop income which might have been obtained from the land had the trees not been there. We estimated that the presence of the trees cut down the crop of beans from the land 30 per cent. As the average net income from beans was $13.35 an acre this would amount to $4 an acre a year--an insignificant sum.

IN BEARING.--Having given the reader an idea of the probable cost of bringing an orchard to bearing age, it may be well also to give the cost of producing apples in a mature apple orchard. Our bearing apple orchard consists of 6.1 acres containing 234 trees. About one-half of the trees, or 110, are 36 years old. The remainder are nearly 50 years of age. As they are all in one block and handled together, the charges cannot well be separated. One hundred and thirty-four of the trees are Baldwins, 44 Twenty Ounce, 40 Tompkins County Kings, and the remainder odd varieties. For the whole period of ten years the orchard has had very good care and attention.

A cover crop was not sown every year, but when it was used the charge was made against the orchard. The manure charge, omitted because of uncertainty as to the exact amount applied and as to its real value, is the only thing lacking in this table.

Two or three sprayings have been made every year. Until 1909, Bordeaux mixture and Paris green were used, but since then the commercial brands of lime sulphur and arsenate of lead have taken their place, nearly doubling the cost of the spray material. The average cost of the material for spraying has been $2.50 per acre, or nearly three and one-half cents per barrel of apples harvested. In 1910 this cost was $3.92 per acre and seven cents a barrel.

TABLE SHOWING THE ITEMS OF EXPENSE IN PRODUCING APPLES IN A SIX ACRE
ORCHARD

Year	Cover crop	Spraying mat.	Bar.	5% int. on inv.	Equip. charge	O'vh'd charge	Labor cost	Total cost
1902		$6.64	$117.88	$27.45	$25.00	$2.97	$339.45	$519.39
1903		11.22	164.92	28.88	25.00	2.88	249.55	482.56
1904		10.50	109.90	30.50	25.00	3.93	180.55	360.38
1905	$6.10	12.45	88.80	30.50	25.00	3.40	158.06	324.31
1906		14.85	112.35	33.06	25.00	4.78	211.76	401.80
1907	10.00	16.85	79.80	35.56	25.00	4.89	192.30	364.40
1908		9.75	205.45	37.76	30.09	5.09	293.50	583.55
1909	8.68	19.26	196.35	41.97	38.98	5.91	280.78	591.93
1910		23.89	116.90	45.75	32.39	5.58	175.26	399.77
1911	10.50	27.08	206.38	45.75	32.39*	5.53*	275.00*	602.63
10 yr. av.	$15.25	$139.87	$35.73	$28.37	$4.78		$235.62	$463.07
Av. per acre	2.50	22.93	5.86	4.65	.78		38.63	75.92
Av. per bbl	.036	.327	.084	.066	.011		.552	-1.08

* Partly estimated, records not yet complete.

The cost of the package has varied from 28 to 38 cents and has averaged about 32 1/2 cents, or $22.93 per acre. Of course the latter amount varies greatly with the crop.

Interest has in all cases been figured at five per cent., but as the price of the land has varied from $90 an acre at the beginning of the period to its present valuation of $160,00 an acre, due both to its improvement and to a general increase in the price of land, the amount of interest has also varied. The same is true of the equipment charge which has steadily increased each year. The average valuation of the land for the ten-year period was $117.15 an acre. This means an annual interest charge of $5.86 per acre, or 81/2 cents a barrel. The equipment charge, which is interest, repairs, and depreciation on the machinery used in the orchard, amounts to more than 61/2 cents a barrel, or $4.65 per acre. Taxes and insurance on the buildings distributed per acre for the farm average $.78 per acre, or a trifle over one cent per barrel. These costs have also increased in the last few years.

Labor is the largest single item. For the first four years this was estimated on the basis of the cost for the last six years, for which more careful records were kept. It is computed at its actual cost to us on the farm, which was 151/2 cents an hour for men and 131/2 cents an hour for horses. This amounts to $4.25 per day for man and team. The cost of the labor to grow, pick, pack, and market a barrel of apples was 55 cents, or $38.63 per acre with an average yield of 70 barrels per acre.

To sum up these items of cost we find that taking the average of ten years with an annual crop of 427 barrels, or 70 per acre, on 6.1 acres of old apple orchard that the costs per barrel have been as follows: spray material, $.036; packages, $.327; interest on the land, $.084; use of equipment, $.066; taxes, $.011; labor, $.552; and a total of $1.08 per barrel. If the estimated cost of manure, six cents a barrel be added, the total will be $1.14. As we have said, these costs per barrel vary with the crop. When our yield was 100 barrels per acre the cost per barrel was only $.99, but when it was 34 barrels per acre this cost rose to $1.73 per barrel. In 1910 we grew a crop of 55 barrels per acre for $1.20 per barrel.

It may be of interest to some to know what the income and profit were on this orchard. For this purpose we give the following table showing the yield, income, cost, and net profit for each of the ten years, and the average:

Year	Yield in bbls. per A.	Income bbls. only	Income inc. culls and drops	Cost per bbl.	Net bbls. alone	Profit inc. culls and drops
1902	103	$1.96*	$1.46*	$.83	$1.13	$.63
1903	71	1.90	2.23	1.11	.79	1.12
1904	51	1.66	1.78	1.15	.51	.63
1905	49	2.30	2.68	1.10	1.20	1.58
1906	53	1.96	2.25	1.25	.71	1.30
1907	34	3.49	4.10	1.73	1.76	2.37
1908	96	2.03	2.32	.99	1.04	1.33
1909	92	3.00	3.38	1.06	1.94	2.32
1910	55	2.69	3.03	1.20	1.49	1.83
1911	100	2.06	2.32	.99¤	1.07¤	1.33¤
10 yr. av.	70	2.15	2.47	1.08	1.07	1.39

* In arriving at these incomes different divisors were used. Two hundred barrels of the crop were sold in bulk and these were not used in getting the average income from barrels only, but were used in getting the average income including culls and drops.

¤ Partly estimated, records not yet being complete for the season.

The Codes Of Hammurabi And Moses
W. W. Davies

QTY

The discovery of the Hammurabi Code is one of the greatest achievements of archaeology, and is of paramount interest, not only to the student of the Bible, but also to all those interested in ancient history...

Religion   **ISBN:** *1-59462-338-4*   **Pages:132**
MSRP $12.95

The Theory of Moral Sentiments
Adam Smith

QTY

This work from 1749. contains original theories of conscience amd moral judgment and it is the foundation for systemof morals.

Philosophy   **ISBN:** *1-59462-777-0*   **Pages:536**
MSRP $19.95

Jessica's First Prayer
Hesba Stretton

QTY

In a screened and secluded corner of one of the many railway-bridges which span the streets of London there could be seen a few years ago, from five o'clock every morning until half past eight, a tidily set-out coffee-stall, consisting of a trestle and board, upon which stood two large tin cans, with a small fire of charcoal burning under each so as to keep the coffee boiling during the early hours of the morning when the work-people were thronging into the city on their way to their daily toil...

Pages:84

Childrens   **ISBN:** *1-59462-373-2*   *MSRP $9.95*

My Life and Work
Henry Ford

QTY

Henry Ford revolutionized the world with his implementation of mass production for the Model T automobile. Gain valuable business insight into his life and work with his own auto-biography... "We have only started on our development of our country we have not as yet, with all our talk of wonderful progress, done more than scratch the surface. The progress has been wonderful enough but..."

Pages:300

Biographies/   **ISBN:** *1-59462-198-5*   *MSRP $21.95*

The Art of Cross-Examination
Francis Wellman

QTY

I presume it is the experience of every author, after his first book is published upon an important subject, to be almost overwhelmed with a wealth of ideas and illustrations which could readily have been included in his book, and which to his own mind, at least, seem to make a second edition inevitable. Such certainly was the case with me; and when the first edition had reached its sixth impression in five months, I rejoiced to learn that it seemed to my publishers that the book had met with a sufficiently favorable reception to justify a second and considerably enlarged edition. ..

Pages:412

Reference   ISBN: *1-59462-647-2*   *MSRP $19.95*

On the Duty of Civil Disobedience
Henry David Thoreau

QTY

Thoreau wrote his famous essay, On the Duty of Civil Disobedience, as a protest against an unjust but popular war and the immoral but popular institution of slave-owning. He did more than write—he declined to pay his taxes, and was hauled off to gaol in consequence. Who can say how much this refusal of his hastened the end of the war and of slavery ?

Law   ISBN: *1-59462-747-9*   **Pages:48**

MSRP $7.45

Dream Psychology Psychoanalysis for Beginners
Sigmund Freud

QTY

Sigmund Freud, born Sigismund Schlomo Freud (May 6, 1856 - September 23, 1939), was a Jewish-Austrian neurologist and psychiatrist who co-founded the psychoanalytic school of psychology. Freud is best known for his theories of the unconscious mind, especially involving the mechanism of repression; his redefinition of sexual desire as mobile and directed towards a wide variety of objects; and his therapeutic techniques, especially his understanding of transference in the therapeutic relationship and the presumed value of dreams as sources of insight into unconscious desires.

Dream Psychology
Psychoanalysis for Beginners

Sigmund Freud

Psychology   ISBN: *1-59462-905-6*   **Pages:196**

MSRP $15.45

The Miracle of Right Thought
Orison Swett Marden

QTY

Believe with all of your heart that you will do what you were made to do. When the mind has once formed the habit of holding cheerful, happy, prosperous pictures, it will not be easy to form the opposite habit. It does not matter how improbable or how far away this realization may see, or how dark the prospects may be, if we visualize them as best we can, as vividly as possible, hold tenaciously to them and vigorously struggle to attain them, they will gradually become actualized, realized in the life. But a desire, a longing without endeavor, a yearning abandoned or held indifferently will vanish without realization.

Pages:360

Self Help   ISBN: *1-59462-644-8*   *MSRP $25.45*

QTY

The Rosicrucian Cosmo-Conception Mystic Christianity by *Max Heindel* ISBN: *1-59462-188-8* **$38.95**
The Rosicrucian Cosmo-conception is not dogmatic, neither does it appeal to any other authority than the reason of the student. It is: not controversial, but is: sent forth in the, hope that it may help to clear... New Age/Religion Pages 646

Abandonment To Divine Providence by *Jean-Pierre de Caussade* ISBN: *1-59462-228-0* **$25.95**
"The Rev. Jean Pierre de Caussade was one of the most remarkable spiritual writers of the Society of Jesus in France in the 18th Century. His death took place at Toulouse in 1751. His works have gone through many editions and have been republished... Inspirational/Religion Pages 400

Mental Chemistry by *Charles Haanel* ISBN: *1-59462-192-6* **$23.95**
Mental Chemistry allows the change of material conditions by combining and appropriately utilizing the power of the mind. Much like applied chemistry creates something new and unique out of careful combinations of chemicals the mastery of mental chemistry... New Age Pages 354

The Letters of Robert Browning and Elizabeth Barret Barrett 1845-1846 vol II ISBN: *1-59462-193-4* **$35.95**
by *Robert Browning* and *Elizabeth Barrett* Biographies Pages 596

Gleanings In Genesis (volume I) by *Arthur W. Pink* ISBN: *1-59462-130-6* **$27.45**
Appropriately has Genesis been termed "the seed plot of the Bible" for in it we have, in germ form, almost all of the great doctrines which are afterwards fully developed in the books of Scripture which follow... Religion/Inspirational Pages 420

The Master Key by *L. W. de Laurence* ISBN: *1-59462-001-6* **$30.95**
In no branch of human knowledge has there been a more lively increase of the spirit of research during the past few years than in the study of Psychology, Concentration and Mental Discipline. The requests for authentic lessons in Thought Control, Mental Discipline and... New Age/Business Pages 422

The Lesser Key Of Solomon Goetia by *L. W. de Laurence* ISBN: *1-59462-092-X* **$9.95**
This translation of the first book of the "Lernegton" which is now for the first time made accessible to students of Talismanic Magic was done, after careful collation and edition, from numerous Ancient Manuscripts in Hebrew, Latin, and French... New Age/Occult Pages 92

Rubaiyat Of Omar Khayyam by *Edward Fitzgerald* ISBN:*1-59462-332-5* **$13.95**
Edward Fitzgerald, whom the world has already learned, in spite of his own efforts to remain within the shadow of anonymity, to look upon as one of the rarest poets of the century, was born at Bredfield, in Suffolk, on the 31st of March, 1809. He was the third son of John Purcell... Music Pages 172

Ancient Law by *Henry Maine* ISBN: *1-59462-128-4* **$29.95**
The chief object of the following pages is to indicate some of the earliest ideas of mankind, as they are reflected in Ancient Law, and to point out the relation of those ideas to modern thought. Religion/History Pages 452

Far-Away Stories by *William J. Locke* ISBN: *1-59462-129-2* **$19.45**
"Good wine needs no bush, but a collection of mixed vintages does. And this book is just such a collection. Some of the stories I do not want to remain buried for ever in the museum files of dead magazine-numbers an author's not unpardonable vanity..." Fiction Pages 272

Life of David Crockett by *David Crockett* ISBN: *1-59462-250-7* **$27.45**
"Colonel David Crockett was one of the most remarkable men of the times in which he lived. Born in humble life, but gifted with a strong will, an indomitable courage, and unremitting perseverance... Biographies/New Age Pages 424

Lip-Reading by *Edward Nitchie* ISBN: *1-59462-206-X* **$25.95**
Edward B. Nitchie, founder of the New York School for the Hard of Hearing, now the Nitchie School of Lip-Reading, Inc, wrote "LIP-READING Principles and Practice". The development and perfecting of this meritorious work on lip-reading was an undertaking... How-to Pages 400

A Handbook of Suggestive Therapeutics, Applied Hypnotism, Psychic Science ISBN: *1-59462-214-0* **$24.95**
by *Henry Munro* Health/New Age/Health/Self-help Pages 376

A Doll's House: and Two Other Plays by *Henrik Ibsen* ISBN: *1-59462-112-8* **$19.95**
Henrik Ibsen created this classic when in revolutionary 1848 Rome. Introducing some striking concepts in playwriting for the realist genre, this play has been studied the world over. Fiction/Classics/Plays 308

The Light of Asia by *sir Edwin Arnold* ISBN: *1-59462-204-3* **$13.95**
In this poetic masterpiece, Edwin Arnold describes the life and teachings of Buddha. The man who was to become known as Buddha to the world was born as Prince Gautama of India but he rejected the worldly riches and abandoned the reigns of power when... Religion/History/Biographies Pages 170

The Complete Works of Guy de Maupassant by *Guy de Maupassant* ISBN: *1-59462-157-8* **$16.95**
"For days and days, nights and nights, I had dreamed of that first kiss which was to consecrate our engagement, and I knew not on what spot I should put my lips..." Fiction/Classics Pages 240

The Art of Cross-Examination by *Francis L. Wellman* ISBN: *1-59462-309-0* **$26.95**
Written by a renowned trial lawyer, Wellman imparts his experience and uses case studies to explain how to use psychology to extract desired information through questioning. How-to/Science/Reference Pages 408

Answered or Unanswered? by *Louisa Vaughan* ISBN: *1-59462-248-5* **$10.95**
Miracles of Faith in China Religion Pages 112

The Edinburgh Lectures on Mental Science (1909) by *Thomas* ISBN: *1-59462-008-3* **$11.95**
This book contains the substance of a course of lectures recently given by the writer in the Queen Street Hall, Edinburgh. Its purpose is to indicate the Natural Principles governing the relation between Mental Action and Material Conditions... New Age/Psychology Pages 148

Ayesha by *H. Rider Haggard* ISBN: *1-59462-301-5* **$24.95**
Verily and indeed it is the unexpected that happens! Probably if there was one person upon the earth from whom the Editor of this, and of a certain previous history, did not expect to hear again... Classics Pages 380

Ayala's Angel by *Anthony Trollope* ISBN: *1-59462-352-X* **$29.95**
The two girls were both pretty, but Lucy who was twenty-one who supposed to be simple and comparatively unattractive, whereas Ayala was credited, as her Bombwhat romantic name might show, with poetic charm and a taste for romance, Ayala when her father died was nineteen... Fiction Pages 484

The American Commonwealth by *James Bryce* ISBN: *1-59462-286-8* **$34.45**
An interpretation of American democratic political theory. It examines political mechanics and society from the perspective of Scotsman James Bryce Politics Pages 572

Stories of the Pilgrims by *Margaret P. Pumphrey* ISBN: *1-59462-116-0* **$17.95**
This book explores pilgrims religious oppression in England as well as their escape to Holland and eventual crossing to America on the Mayflower, and their early days in New England... History Pages 268

www.bookjungle.com *email: sales@bookjungle.com fax: 630-214-0564 mail: Book Jungle PO Box 2226 Champaign, IL 61825*

QTY

The Fasting Cure *by Sinclair Upton*　　　　　　　　　　　　　　ISBN: *1-59462-222-1*　**$13.95**
In the Cosmopolitan Magazine for May, 1910, and in the Contemporary Review (London) for April, 1910, I published an article dealing with my experiences in fasting. I have written a great many magazine articles, but never one which attracted so much attention... New Age/Self Help/Health Pages 164

Hebrew Astrology *by Sepharial*　　　　　　　　　　　　　　　ISBN: *1-59462-308-2*　**$13.45**
In these days of advanced thinking it is a matter of common observation that we have left many of the old landmarks behind and that we are now pressing forward to greater heights and to a wider horizon than that which represented the mind-content of our progenitors...　Astrology Pages 144

Thought Vibration or The Law of Attraction in the Thought World　　ISBN: *1-59462-127-6*　**$12.95**
by William Walker Atkinson　　　　　　　　　　　　　　　　　　　*Psychology/Religion Pages 144*

Optimism *by Helen Keller*　　　　　　　　　　　　　　　　　ISBN: *1-59462-108-X*　**$15.95**
Helen Keller was blind, deaf, and mute since 19 months old, yet famously learned how to overcome these handicaps, communicate with the world, and spread her lectures promoting optimism. An inspiring read for everyone...　Biographies/Inspirational Pages 84

Sara Crewe *by Frances Burnett*　　　　　　　　　　　　　　　ISBN: *1-59462-360-0*　**$9.45**
In the first place, Miss Minchin lived in London. Her home was a large, dull, tall one, in a large, dull square, where all the houses were alike, and all the sparrows were alike, and where all the door-knockers made the same heavy sound...　Childrens/Classic Pages 88

The Autobiography of Benjamin Franklin *by Benjamin Franklin*　　　ISBN: *1-59462-135-7*　**$24.95**
The Autobiography of Benjamin Franklin has probably been more extensively read than any other American historical work, and no other book of its kind has had such ups and downs of fortune. Franklin lived for many years in England, where he was agent...　Biographies/History Pages 332

Name	
Email	
Telephone	
Address	
City, State ZIP	

☐ **Credit Card**　　　　　　　☐ **Check / Money Order**

Credit Card Number	
Expiration Date	
Signature	

Please Mail to:　Book Jungle
　　　　　　　　PO Box 2226
　　　　　　　　Champaign, IL 61825
　or Fax to:　　630-214-0564

ORDERING INFORMATION

web*: www.bookjungle.com*
email*: sales@bookjungle.com*
fax*: 630-214-0564*
mail*: Book Jungle PO Box 2226 Champaign, IL 61825*
or PayPal *to sales@bookjungle.com*

Please contact us for bulk discounts

DIRECT-ORDER TERMS

**20% Discount if You Order
Two or More Books**
Free Domestic Shipping!
Accepted: Master Card, Visa,
Discover, American Express